Never a SAINT

POLISHED P&P
SERIES

CHAPTER ONE
KYLO

My knee bounced up and down as I sat across from Saint at his co-owned business, the Polished Pussies and Penises. I'd seen his ad in the paper recruiting men to join the forces for male and female clients in the brothel side of things, but they were branching out into providing an escort service. I'd be happy to do either. I was there to apply for the job. I just wasn't sure he'd accept me since I was a prospect for the Diamond MC that we were both a part of. I was full to the damn brim with nerves, but the money I could make would set me up for life. I never wanted to struggle like I had when I was young and in the hands of my fucked-up parents. If Boom, another member of the MC and an old friend of my father's, hadn't got me out of my hellhole, hadn't taken me in, I would have been messed up for life. I was one of the lucky ones really. There were many out in the world in the same boat I'd been in before Boom took control.

"Are you sure this is what you want?" Saint asked, yet again. He leaned back in his office chair and eyed me like I'd gone insane.

Maybe I had. But the need to set my life up so I could breathe easy and never struggle would be worth it. The current job I had at the gym paid well, but this would pay better, and that was what I felt I needed.

Besides, I loved sex with both men and women. I didn't see the problem with wanting to apply. Hell, it could be a job I would excel at.

"Yeah," I said.

Saint's brows quirked. "You do understand the position, right?"

I stopped myself from rolling my eyes. "Yes."

Saint's lips thinned. "You would have to go on dates with clients lookin' for some company. Then there's the ones who will come here wantin' to fuck." He paused for effect, maybe. "*Men* and women."

That time I did roll my eyes. "You already know I don't care if it's *men* or women. I'm applyin' for the job. I know the details. What are you worried about? That it'll be bad for the Diamond MC?"

Saint shook his head. "Fuck, if anythin', it'll make the club more popular with the women, and the brothers won't give a shit because they're all about money and sex, which is what this job is."

"Exactly."

Saint sighed. "What happens if a man or a woman comes here and you don't find them attractive? Would you still be able to get hard?"

Was he serious? "Yeah, I won't have a problem."

Saint jerked his head back in shock. "Serious?"

"All I gotta do is close my eyes and picture someone I'm into, and if I can't close my eyes, I'll make sure the customer is happily satisfied while I get hard."

He seemed skeptical over my answer. I was only twenty-three and fucking horny, to the point where it was as if I was just learning to use my dick. I'd do just about anyone if it led to me getting off.

"All right." He nodded and then glanced down at the paper in front of him. "Then how would you rate your ability to help your partner find their release?"

I shrugged. I didn't want to brag, but I was after this job after all. "Ten outta ten."

Saint snorted. "Serious?"

I laughed. "You seem to be sayin' that a lot."

His eyes narrowed. No other brother would I have given lip to, but I was good friends with Lucas, Saint's younger, gay brother. So, in a way, I had a feeling I could get away with it a little. However, it might not last because Lucas didn't know I was applying for the job to become a male escort-slash-prostitute. When he'd heard I'd been thinking about it and asked me, I'd told him it'd just been something I was thinking of, that it probably wouldn't happen. Yet, here I was. When Lucas did find out, I expected a lengthy phone call. I just didn't know if he would want to talk me out of it or just need to understand the whys of my choice. I hoped for the second one as I appreciated Lucas's friendship and wouldn't want to lose it over something like this.

I wiped my sweaty palms down my thighs. "No woman or man has left my bed without findin' their own release. I take care of my partners."

He studied me for a moment before looking back down to the sheet of paper. "What would you do if a married couple asks for you and the husband wants to watch you fuck his wife?"

"I would make sure both involved were comfortable around me first, and then I'd find out what's good or bad in the situation, what the husband wouldn't want me to do, and make sure I never stepped over the boundaries."

He nodded. "Who do you prefer, men or women?"

"Either. I'm not picky."

Saint ran a hand over his face. "How do you think Lucas will take this?"

"In the end, I'm hopin' he'll accept my choice. If he's the person I think he is, I reckon he will."

"Prospect—"

I shook my head. "I think in here you can call me Kylo."

He eyed me again, and I really wanted to know what was running through his pretty head. "Kylo." His jaw clenched. "No brother should have to be paid to have sex to get some action between the sheets."

I clutched my stomach as I laughed hard. "You… think… I'm doin' this to get sex?" I shook my head. "Saint, no. I can get any whenever I want. I'm doin' this for the money and the fact I enjoy sex helps. Which I'm sure you understand. I've heard about your endeavors."

"Whatever." He glared. "I just need to make sure you're *definitely* okay with male clients."

I ran my still sweaty hands down my thighs again. I never did well in a room with Saint because I'd always been attracted to the guy. He made me nervous a lot of the times where I would just say whatever.

"Saint, I can and have made a guy come in minutes with just my mouth. I'll be fine with male clients." Jesus, did I have to say it like that? It was true, but still, it had me sounding cocky. I wasn't. I just knew how to give good head. Huh, maybe I was cocky.

Saint scoffed. "You can't be that fuckin' good." He picked up a pen and wrote something down.

"What are you writin'?"

"Nothin'," he replied with a smirk.

"Saint, what did you write?"

"That you're adequate in bed."

Now that just pissed me off. *Adequate.* I wasn't that. I was a damn bomb. "I could make you come in a few minutes," I told him, raising a brow in challenge, even while in my head, I screamed, *What the fuck you think you're doin'? He's a brother.* If I thought I was sweaty before, it upped a notch, my neck already damp.

The room was damn quiet.

So fucking quiet as we stared at each other.

Saint finally snorted. "I doubt you could."

"Then let me prove it." *Shut the fuck up, man. He will kick your ass.*

More silence. I hated silence. I wanted to say awkward shit when there was nothing but silence between people. Shit, too late. I'd already said awkward crap.

Had I really offered to suck Saint's dick to prove I rocked with my blow job techniques?

Yes. Yes, I damn well had, and now I felt like I was going to piss myself because he was still sitting there staring at me. But I couldn't seem to look away either.

Fuck me, we were on the road to disaster and I couldn't jump off.

Who was I kidding? He wouldn't take me up on my offer. Suddenly, I relaxed and laughed silently in my mind. I was overreacting for nothing. This was Saint I propositioned. The man was known for the women he slept with. He wouldn't want a guy near his junk.

I was an idiot to even suggest it, but even worse for getting nervous and feeling awkward over it because it wouldn't happen, which would be the best for both of us.

I opened my mouth to tell him to forget it, but he got there first with "Fine. Show me."

Wait… what?

I stuck a finger in each ear and shook it around. I was obviously hearing things. But when Saint still stared at me, only now with his own smirk, I knew I hadn't imagined it.

Still, I had to check. "What did you say?"

He snorted. "Show me."

He did say it. He wanted me to show him my skills.

What the fuck?

Saint pushed his chair away from the desk, swung it to the side, and gestured down to his dick. "Well?"

Holy shit. Holy, holy shit. I was about to suck Saint's dick. I'd dreamed of this. I'd masturbated to this.

Fucking hell, do not say anything stupid. I thinned my lips and stood. Christ, my knees shook, but I kept my face stoic, at least I hoped I did, as I walked toward his desk. On the inside, I was freaking the fuck out. What happened after this? How would we act? He'd be my boss and I'd be working for him fucking people.

This was a bad idea.

I stopped. "You know what, maybe you should just trust me on my skills?"

His smile was wicked when he reached down and popped the button on his jeans. "Chickenin' out?"

Shit, fuck, dick.

I wasn't one to knock back a challenge and knew Saint was as stubborn as I was. Maybe I should have brought up the after-the-moment situation. Maybe I should have been smarter than him and walked out of the room, forgetting this and forgetting about the job.

However, I never said I was smart.

Walking around the desk, I dropped to my knees and hoped when Saint saw me there, he would freak out and stop this.

He didn't.

Then I realized he was probably picturing I was some woman. Yeah, that made sense. No doubt he would close his eyes and think it was a woman's mouth around him.

All right then, I could do this.

It was for the job and to show my skills.

I could suck Saint off.

Fuck… it was Saint.

Maybe I had to close my eyes and think of someone else.

For some stupid reason, I clapped my hands and rubbed them together. "Right, let's do this," I said like we were going to play a sport or cards.

Saint didn't say anything; he just dipped his chin down at his junk. The bastard wasn't going to back out. All right then, I would blow his fucking mind. Reaching out, I fisted my hands so he didn't see them shake. He leaned back enough I could grab the top of his jeans in one hand and use the other to unzip them.

He still said nothing, so I guessed it was go time.

I slid my hand in and was surprised to find him half hard already when I pulled him free of his jeans and boxers. He'd probably been thinking of his current lay. Or it could have been the talk of sucking. I knew I was also sporting an erection because of all the chatting.

This was it.

I could do this. I was confident in my skills. I just hoped the prick didn't hold off his release by thinking of a naked granny or something.

"Just… close your eyes and feel. No funny shit like thinkin' of somethin' disgustin'," I told him with a glare.

His eyes narrowed right back. "I'll be fuckin' honest."

"Right." I nodded once.

"Good."

"Fine," I clipped.

Saint rolled his eyes. "Just get to work already before I die of boredom."

"Fuck you," I snarled.

Saint snorted. "No thanks, not into guys. I'm just proving a point."

"So am I."

"Great, then get to it… unless you want to forget this and say I win?"

I wanted to punch that smug grin off his damn beautiful face. "Bullshit, I'm not givin' in."

He waved a hand around and then rested it, like his other one, on the arm of his chair. I wished he'd look away, and then my gut wouldn't be playing havoc and my heart wouldn't be dancing around in my chest like it'd just taken a sniff of coke.

"Condom?" I asked.

"I'm clean." He pulled open a drawer and put his test results on the desk.

"Do you usually show your women this before—"

He glared. "No, I'm usually gloved to the nines."

What did that mean? Holy fuck, did he usually wear a condom

when getting head? Then why wasn't he here in this situation? What the fuck did it mean?

I had to push that thought away or I wouldn't be able to perform since my mind would be busy questioning everything. *Shut your mind down, Kylo,* I told myself. "Well, you've seen my test." It was something I had to have before I even applied for the job, and I hadn't been with anyone since. Had Saint? Nope, I had to forget that thought also. Did I trust him with the results? Yeah, I did. He wouldn't fuck with that type of thing.

He grunted and arched a brow as if to say get on with it.

Fine then. I nodded once again, leaned in, and licked around the tip of Saint's cock. It twitched, perking up from the attention. I went to the side and ran my tongue and lips up and down his length, while I snuck a look up at him to see if his eyes were closed.

They weren't.

Dammit.

I closed mine and licked back up to the tip, swirling my tongue around the edge again before taking him into my mouth and gliding down along his long, thick length. I ignored the breath he hissed out and got down to business. I bobbed up and down on him, making sure to use my tongue and lips. Reaching in, I cupped his balls and rolled them gently around. He sucked in a breath. Opening my eyes, I saw his grip on the arms of his chair tighten. After licking the outside and all around, I went back to the tip and stuck my tongue in the slit, where I tasted precum.

Christ, I was rock-hard in my jeans and wanted to take it out and jack off, but it wasn't the time or place, even though I had a dick in my mouth. I was there to prove a point.

I sucked him all the way into my mouth, where he touched the back of my throat, and I opened wider, drawing in more, gagging only a little.

"Fuck," Saint whispered.

I would have smiled if I wasn't busy sucking, licking, and taking his cock in my mouth over and over again.

"Kylo," Saint started, and my dick throbbed from hearing my name drop from his mouth with desire in his voice. "Close," he added. I sucked him in deep again and moaned around him. That was when I felt him jerk in my mouth. He groaned low as his cum shot into the back of my throat and I swallowed it down as it kept coming.

When he relaxed back in the chair, I withdrew my mouth and used my hand to draw out the last of his cum and then licked it off the tip before sitting back on my knees. I glanced at the clock on the wall behind his desk. "Three minutes."

He stared at me like he'd never seen me before.

He probably hadn't. I was just a prospect to the club and his brother's friend.

Now I was also someone who he'd come down the throat of.

And here was the awkward part.

As I stood, I discreetly adjusted my aching cock and went back around his desk to sit in the chair again. I could have put his dick away, but then I probably wouldn't have let go of it. I liked sucking him off. A little too much.

Jesus Christ, I was screwed.

No. Fuck no. I wouldn't let this moment get to me. After all, if I got the job, which I knew I would after making him come so quickly, I could busy my mind with other people—the clients.

Saint cleared his throat. I glanced up to see him standing and slowly putting his dick away. I gulped, and my dick pulsed once more. I needed a release.

I shifted my gaze up to find Saint watching me with a smug smile on his face. The prick knew he'd affected me. He did that little show to see where I would look, and I'd just shown all my cards. Yeah, I wouldn't mind his dick in my mouth again, but I wouldn't ever get it.

Somewhere there were doves crying over the matter.

"Do I get the job?" I asked.

He nodded. "Give me the times you'll be working at the compound and we'll work around it."

I stood again and slipped a piece of paper out the back of my pocket. I'd already thought he would need it. I placed it on his desk and said, "See you Friday. That's when I can start."

"I'll have something set up for you."

My gut sank. I thought I wanted this. Now I wasn't so sure, but I wouldn't back down.

There was enough evidence to say I wasn't gay, but fuck me sideways, I enjoyed Kylo sucking me off in my office the other day. I didn't think he'd do it, but it just proved that when two stubborn people wouldn't back down, things happened.

Now that scene pushed into my mind at the weirdest moments. When I was taking a piss, cooking, eating, when I was fucking a random, and when I was lying in bed waiting for sleep to take me.

I hadn't seen him since that day and he'd be in shortly for his first job. I wasn't sure I wanted to see him. This shit felt strange and I wasn't used to feeling uncomfortable, yet horny at the same time.

And seriously, why the hell did I get head without protection? I'd never done that, and I kept trying to tell myself it was for the experience of receiving my first blow job off a guy, but I wasn't so sure. My head was a mess.

A knock sounded on my door. It was my door, even though I co-owned with Country, State, and Wreck, but they had an office on the top floor. We each took a turn at managing this local club and oversaw the other clubs via calls, emails, and videos with the others we'd opened.

"Enter," I called.

It opened and in stepped Lucas, my brother. My eyes widened. "What are *you* doin' here?" He'd never dropped into Polished before, why now?

"A little birdy told me that Kylo has his first job tonight."

I snorted. "A little birdy? Do you mean that guy you call your boyfriend?"

"Maybe." He smiled. It was good to see him happy. Never thought it would be with a brother, but Wreck proved he cared for Lucas as much as Lucas adored him. It was strange, but who was I to stop something that was obviously good for each of them? Even when I was pissed after finding out they'd been seeing each other behind my back, and that, at first, I didn't trust Wreck playing with my brother's heart. It took only moments to see Wreck was real about it all, which was after I'd hit him in the face.

Now they just made me sick with all the loving they had going on for each other.

"Why come here for Kylo?"

"The... *idiot* hasn't been taking my calls or returning my texts ever since I found out he had an interview here. *And* this is after he told me at the first compound party I went to that he wasn't really going to apply. I thought I'd catch him here since he's also been dodging me everywhere else."

"Bro, I don't think here is the right place. What happens if you mess with his head and he can't do what he's gotta do?" Not that Kylo had an appointment for sex that night. I hadn't booked him in for one, but he did have a date with a rich woman who just wanted company while out to dinner. Could I have made an appointment for him with a woman or man for sex? Yeah, we were picking up in that direction, but the others we'd hired would be doing that tonight. They'd had previous experience in selling themselves in the bedroom... well, except for West, Lucas's friend from college, but he was another who would be just going out on a date for company.

"I'm not here to judge. You know me better than that. I just want to tell him to stop evading me. I don't like it." His smile disappeared and he looked to the ground. Yeah, Lucas wouldn't like that happening. He didn't have many friends and losing the ones he had would hurt him.

"All right, just sit tight. He should be here soon. He has to come in here for his appointment card."

Lucas's smile was back. "Thanks." He'd made it to the seat across from my desk when another knock sounded on my door.

"Enter," I called.

The door opened and West poked his head in. "Hey—Lucas," West called, his voice higher than I'd heard it before. "What are you doing here?" West stepped through the door, closed it, and leaned against the wooden panel. He looked pale.

Fuck. Not another one who hadn't said shit to people. Sighing, I dropped my head back and then stood.

"A-Are you working here?" Lucas asked.

West gulped. He looked at me, and I nodded toward Lucas, trying to tell him he needed to explain this to my brother. West rubbed a hand over his face and moved over to lean his ass on my damn desk as he faced Lucas.

"Shit, ah, yes, I'm working here. The job I had wasn't paying enough and they cut my hours back. I needed a new job that paid well with hours that suited me. This was it."

"But… you're willing to sleep with people for it?" Lucas asked; then he noticed what he said and his hands shot up. "Not that I'm judging because I'm not. It's just… I mean… um, that… ah, I thought you've only ever been with one guy."

West smiled. "I have, but it doesn't mean we didn't do a lot of things. Things that I enjoyed. Plus, Saint promised he wouldn't have me be with anyone shady."

"We're starting out slow," I offered. "I'm only sending him out on dates where a man is looking for company, not sex. Yet."

Lucas nodded. "Okay, that's good, and I'm sure the men will love you because you're handsome."

"Can I tell Wreck you said that?" I asked. Lucas glared and I chuckled. Wreck was damn protective of Lucas. He didn't like anyone looking at him or talking to him if he thought they wanted a piece of him. He also wasn't a fan of Lucas saying shit like that. I just thought it was hilarious and often teased them about it.

"He'll know I didn't mean anything by it," Lucas said.

I raised a brow.

"He will," Lucas stated. I grinned. "Oh, shut up, you." Lucas looked back to West. "I'm upset with you."

"Because I didn't tell you what's going on and now this?"

"Exactly."

"I know. I'd be pissed as well if it was you. I just didn't want to spoil what was happening between you and Wreck. I didn't want to be a downer."

"Stop it. No matter when or where, you can come to me. I'm always here for you." Lucas suddenly sat straighter. Crap, he'd had an idea and I wasn't sure it would be good for Wreck in the end. "I know. You should come live with Wreck and me for a little while when we move into the new place in about a month." Lucas could see West was about to say no, so he went on. "It'll be cheaper than where you are now and closer to the college. The house is *huge*." He waved his hand out and around him. "We won't be in each other's way at all."

Nope, Wreck would hate this idea, but knowing the punk-ass, he'd give in for Lucas.

"Lucas, thank you for the offer, but—"

"Don't say no yet. Think about it. Come by tomorrow night for dinner and we'll talk some more. Please?" As soon as he pouted and I saw West thawing, I knew West would agree.

"Fine." He sighed. "But can we make it Sunday night?"

"Deal." Lucas grinned.

Another knock sounded, and my goddamn heart gave a hard thump.

"Enter," I said.

I already knew who it was, and fuck me, I wasn't ready to see him and his lips, or mouth, or tongue.

The door swung open and Kylo stepped through. His smile was hesitant before it vanished when he saw Lucas sitting in the chair. He glanced at me and scowled, as if it was my fault he'd been dodging my brother and that Lucas had to resort to showing up here just to have a word with him.

I rolled my eyes so I could get a quick look at his junk to see if he was hard. He was. It had my mind jumping straight to wondering if he was hard because he had to come in here to see me. Had he been thinking of sucking me? I'd noticed he was hard after he'd proved he could make a guy come in minutes. He'd enjoyed it, and my body appealed to him. And when I stretched after receiving head, his gaze had run over me and stopped on my dick. At that moment, he'd looked at it like he wanted more.

Shit. I quickly sat back down to hide the fact my dick thought it was preening time. It started thickening, listening in on my thoughts.

"What are you doin' here, Lucas?" Kylo asked from the still-open doorway.

"Close the door," I ordered.

His jaw clenched, and he didn't look at me, but he did as I asked. Kylo glanced at West, then Lucas again.

"So you know he's workin' here as well?"

"I do." Lucas nodded. "Now, I want to know why you've been hiding from me."

"Because I couldn't stand it if you didn't accept this. It'd make me feel like the shittiest person. You won't understand my reasonin'. You have great parents, and you know I didn't. Drugs were their life." He laughed without humor. "There were days they had no money for food and I had to go without. When they didn't pay the power bills, I went without light in that hovel of a place. When they didn't pay the gas, there was no hot water. I never had a lot until Boom took me in. I don't ever want to feel that again in my life, so I'm making sure I'll have money to set me up. This is a fuckin' good payin' job."

Kylo looked away from my brother. He seemed disappointed, not by Lucas, but in himself, and I wanted to stand in front of him and protect him.

Wait… what the fuck? No, I didn't. I shook my head at the ridiculous thought.

Still, I felt bad for him, and what he'd said made a lot of sense.

"Kylo," Lucas whispered. I ground my teeth together, not understanding the feeling from hearing my brother say Kylo's name like that. Lucas stood and made his way across the room to Kylo, who he pulled into a hug. I stretched my neck side to side, suddenly feeling tense.

"You never have to justify yourself to anyone. Be who you want, do what you want, and you'll always have my friendship."

"Mine too," West added.

Kylo put his arms around Lucas's shoulders since my brother took after our mom, who was damn short. My gut clenched, and I put it down to hunger.

I clapped my hands. Immediately, they startled and moved apart, all of them looking at me. "Now we know it's all good, can I get down to business?"

"Right," Lucas started. "Yes, of course. Anyway, Wade will be waiting for me. I better go."

I shook my head. It was yet another strange thing, hearing my brother call Wreck by his real name. We'd been brothers of the Dimond MC for years and I'd never used his real name.

"Talk soon," Lucas called as he slipped out the door and closed it after himself.

"West, here's your information about tonight. You'll have clothes set out in room 203, and you'll be expected at the Bell Apartments by seven."

"Okay." He nodded, coming forward to grab the sheet of paper. "All right, I can do this…. It is just dinner?"

I gave him a smile. "Yeah, man. Just dinner and your company, which you'll be paid well for. Until you get used to it."

"Cool," he said, and as he walked to the door, he said to Kylo, "Good luck tonight."

"You too, West." Kylo gently punched him in the arm before West walked out. Kylo looked back at me. "What you got for me, boss?"

Was it the lighting in here, or were his cheeks a little redder?

I grabbed his piece of paper and held it out. He walked closer, took it, and read the information.

"A woman named Fiona in her fifties, looking for some company while out to dinner." He flipped it over and then lifted his head. "That's it?"

"Yep. Just take her out to dinner and woo her."

"Nothing after it?"

"No."

"But…."

"Your clothes are in room 405. There you'll also find keys to a Chrysler. You'll pick her up at the address provided by 8:00 p.m. She likes late dinners. I've booked you in fifteen minutes after pick-up at Le Cirque. Be on your best behavior."

His jaw clenched. "You didn't say that to West when he left."

"What?" I asked, leaning forward to rest my elbows on the desk.

"Be on your best behavior." He must have registered that he sounded like a teenager because he quickly added, "Forget it."

"Kylo," I called when he started for the door. He turned back. "You and West are the least experienced in selling your body. I have others who have done it for years to pick up those clients… for now. You'll be watched like all employees are when they leave our premises. If I hear good things about the way you work with the client, then you'll be put into a different position. Until then, you and West will be having the same details each time."

He nodded and faced the door again.

"Kylo," I called, and I wasn't sure why I did it. When he looked over his shoulder, I added, "You understand my choice?"

"Yes, boss."

"Good, then you can go."

He did and the room quieted when he closed the door after himself. I knew outside that door people were working their asses off by either taking clients to their rooms or off getting ready for one. The other co-owners had wanted their office far away from the action, which was why they picked the top floor, but I wanted mine right in the mix of things. It was soundproof when the door was closed, but as soon as it opened, I heard it all. I also liked not being far from the front entrance in case there was a problem. Yeah, we had other brothers who took care of the security details, but I was always willing to help out when things got difficult.

I picked up my phone and pressed in a contact. "Saint," Torch answered.

"You've got Kylo tonight, and tell Death he's on West. Both are dates only, but you never know what can happen."

"Got it, but who the fuck is Kylo?"

I rolled my eyes. "The prospect." Kylo didn't have a club name until he graduated to a full member. Until then, we only knew him as the prospect, like the other few wanting to be a part of the club.

"Which one?" he asked.

I sighed and heard Death say something in the background. Torch made a noise. "Right, the one who's your brother's friend."

"Yeah, him."

The one who sucked my dick like no one had before.

"What room is he in?" Torch asked.

"Room 405, and tell Death that West is in 203, but he won't be there long. He'll need to move his ass to get there."

"On it. Recon later," Torch said and then hung up.

"Fuck," I clipped, after I dropped the phone to my desk. I scrubbed a hand over my face and slouched. I'd lied to West and Kylo. Out of the other men we'd hired, only one had experience. The other five hadn't. However, since Kylo and West were my brother's friends, I would hold them off as long as I could before moving them into the other position.

At least, that was what I was telling myself about Kylo anyway.

CHAPTER THREE
KYLO

As I got dressed in a suit and tie, I tried to calm my jitters. At least things with Lucas were properly sorted; it would be good to have him back in my life since I didn't need to dodge him anymore. Only that thought drifted from my mind because my nerves were taking control. I couldn't help but think things would have been fine if I hadn't seen Saint. I wouldn't be a jumble of goddamn nerves and feel like I would vomit any second. But I was feeling anxious—not over the job I was about to do. I could woo a woman of any age—my skills were just that on point—but fucking hell, seeing Saint messed with me. There was no doubt he'd be on my mind for the night, and not my job.

Shit, I just had to switch my mind off and *stop* thinking about him.

About his dick.

About how he tasted, felt, and sounded when I took him in my mouth.

Fuck.

Yeah, not thinking about him wasn't working too well. It hadn't been ever since it happened. I'd lost count of the times I'd jacked off to the memory, and of course, my mind added some other images to the pictures playing in my head.

But I couldn't think of it now. I was already hard, and I needed my dick to go down, or the client could get a different message. It was weird that I wasn't nervous about meeting this woman. Yet, I'd been close to having a heart attack when I'd knocked on Saint's office door.

Shaking my head, I grabbed the keys from the bedside table and pocketed them along with the one to the room. I took the jacket from the bed and hooked it over my arm as I made my way to the door. Opening it, I jumped and yelled, "Fuck!" when I saw Torch standing on the other side.

He smirked and lifted his chin in greeting along with "Hey."

"What's up?" I asked.

His hand shot out. "Clip this to your suit. It's an alarm. Hit it if something happens and I'll be in to help get you out."

When I didn't take it, he looked up. "What?"

"Seriously?" I had no clue this was how the club worked, and I didn't understand why. "Employees actually need this and the security?"

"Fuck yeah." He reached out and clipped the little pin to the suit. He then turned and started down the hall. He glanced back and said, "Get movin', prospect, and I'll explain things on the way down to the car."

I did, quickly shutting and locking the door behind me. It looked like the room was meant to be mine since the key had been in it when I arrived, so I pocketed it now and raced after Torch.

"We learned early on that the security for Polished had to be top. We got taught that after a bad fuckin' mistake where a woman of ours was assaulted. The guy who'd done it paid. Now we make sure it never happens again. The girls have alarms in their rooms and when they're out of the club, they take alarms that'll ring to the guard appointed to them for the night. I'm it for you tonight. It might be a harmless date with an older woman, but we can never be sure, so it's better to be safe than fuckin' sorry. Get me?"

"Totally."

"Good. I'll be in my own vehicle and I'll follow you to pick her up, then to the restaurant. I don't leave your side until you're back here and done for the night. You do not fuckin' mess around with the rules, because one day, it could cost you. More importantly, it could cost the club, and we won't take a hit over an employee being fuckin' stupid."

"Got it." I nodded.

"Right. It's damn different having you in the MC and workin' here, but we'll get it sorted, so everything runs smoothly. When you're not workin' here, Country said you still have shifts manning the bar at the compound. Saint will have it worked out so they don't clash. Trust Saint, trust your guard, and things'll be goddamn grand."

"Again, got it."

He nodded as we got into the elevator, and he turned to me and stared.

"What?" I asked.

"You sure this is a job you want?"

I smiled. "I'll be doin' this for a few years and then be lookin' at something else. Just want some good money behind me."

"Fair enough, but, prospect, you understand a lot of the clients are lonely and aren't that good-lookin'?"

I laughed. "Yeah, I expected. Still, everyone deserves some lovin' no matter what they look like. Shit, if I could help them out and make their day a little better, then I'd be happy with that."

He looked at me as if he'd only just seen me or met me. I was getting that a lot these days.

"You're a good kid," he said when we walked out of the elevator and into the underground garage.

I snorted. "Torch, how old are you?"

"Thirty."

"I'm twenty-three. I'm not a kid."

He chuckled. "You're still a kid in my eyes, and shit, you look younger. Way younger. It'll be good for business at least." He stopped and turned to me. "Take out your keys to the car and press the button, so you know which one it is. I'll follow at a distance. Good luck, prospect."

"Thanks, Torch." I nodded, and he walked off to his car while I pulled the keys free and went to the vehicle.

As I slid into the seat, I read the address off the sheet. I knew the area, so I'd be able to find it easy enough. Then I checked her name again. "Fiona Martin." I'd have to ask her how she wished to be addressed. I put the sheet in the glove box and started the car. I caught Torch following me out of the underground garage and onto the street.

Most would think this whole gig would be something to get nervous about. Maybe I would have been if it was a real date, but I reminded myself enough that this was business, and it seemed to be sticking. Though, I'd wait and see if I was still this calm when I pulled up out front of the client's house.

Thinking of a house put my mind on where I lived. Boom and Wendy took me in when I was fourteen. They were more my parents than my real ones had been. It was hard to tell them my decision. I worried more about Wendy than Boom because she was the sensitive type, but we'd sworn to always tell each other the truth. Which was also how they knew I was bisexual. However, when the time came, just before the interview, I'd sat them down and explained my reasons for it.

"You know you don't have to do this. We'll help with your future," Wendy had said.

I smiled softly at her. "I know, Wendy, but I want to do this for myself. And if I get the job, I'd also like to pay more rent."

"Boy," Boom boomed—it was how he got his club name; there was nothing quiet about him. "You do what you feel you gotta do, but you'd better wrap it before you tap anything."

He'd said just about the same when I'd told him I was bisexual. God, I loved them. They were the best, and I wanted to give back to them as much as they gave. Boom was nearing sixty, and I was hoping with the extra cash coming in from me, he'd slow down a bit. It was doubtful, as he liked to keep busy, but he'd also promised Wendy a trip away soon, and the money I contributed could make it happen sooner.

I stopped the car out front of a two-story, modern brick home that shouted money. Before nerves even had the chance to surface, I shut the car down and climbed out. I stopped at the gate out front and glanced at the brick fence where there was an intercom.

Pressing the button, I waited.

"Hello?"

"Hi, this is…" Shit, fuck, shit, was I supposed to use my real name? I couldn't remember what the paper said. "Sorry, this is Jack Dell. I'm here to pick up Fiona Martin for dinner." Hell, I would have to remember the name I used so I could use it if she asked for me again. I repeated it over and over in my mind.

"Yes, I'm Fiona Martin. I'll be out in a moment. Thank you."

"Great, see you soon." I wasn't a dick. I didn't go back and wait in the car. Instead, I stayed where I was to escort her there.

The front door opened, and Fiona stepped out. She was dressed in an elegant yet simple black dress with a shawl wrapped around her shoulders and a purse hanging off her arm. As she grew closer, I saw her hair was brown with a few strands of gray peeking through. She was short and plus size, but beautiful.

"Jack, it's lovely to meet you," she greeted at the gate as she unlocked it.

I helped her open it with a smile. "Likewise, Fiona. I'm looking forward to dinner. I haven't had a chance to go there yet."

Her nervous smile brightened. "Oh, it's beautiful."

"I know I'll enjoy it then." I took her hand after she relocked her gate and tucked it into my elbow. I led her to the car and opened her door, but before she got in, I asked, "May I ask what you would prefer I call you?"

She blushed. "Well, you are very young, maybe Mrs. Martin. But then again, it would probably make me feel like I'm speaking to a student. Really, Fiona will be fine."

I grinned. "Anything, Fiona."

"Thank you, Jack."

The drive went smoothly. We chatted every now and then, and it didn't feel uncomfortable. Although, I could sense she was a little hesitant to open up, so I kept it to mundane questions.

Pulling up in front of the restaurant where the valet was, I quickly got out and made my way around the car. I chucked the keys to the guy who'd helped Fiona out of the car and then tucked Fiona's hand back into the crook of my arm. However, she gently pulled it back out. I wasn't sure why, but I didn't let my confusion show. Instead, I placed my hand at the small of her back and guided her in.

Once we were seated and the waitress had taken our drink order, Fiona leaned in and said, "I'm sorry about before. I thought it would look strange if we walked in with me on your arm."

I tilted my head to the side, still confused. "Why?"

Her eyes widened. "Jack, you're young and very handsome. People will wonder what you're doing with someone like me. I… I'm not comfortable having people's judgment. If it seems innocent, like you're my son taking his mother out, then I'll be okay with that."

I played with the stem of the empty wineglass on the table. "Fiona, may I ask why you want company with someone young? You could have asked for any age, but you didn't."

She looked around us, her cheeks heating once more. "Because… well, you see…." She stilled as she glanced over my shoulder. I took a quick look to see a man around Fiona's age with a woman much younger. One who didn't even look twenty-one. Yet, apparently, I didn't look much older either.

However, now I understood what this was about. "Is he your ex?" I asked.

Tears welled and she nodded, looking away from her ex quickly. I wanted to get up and stalk over there to punch the fucker in the face. "Fiona," I said gently and reached out to take her hand in mine. She looked up at me. "I hope you'll believe what I say next, because I promise I'm not saying it considering our agreement." She nodded. I ran my thumb over her hand, back and forth. I smiled. "A lot of men are fools. They don't know when they have something good until they let it go, but even then, sometimes they still don't understand just what they've lost. They'll chase what they think they want for the rest of their lives, and it won't be until the end they realize they had the right person all along, but they'd let them go. Even with the short time I've been in your presence, I know your ex will be one of those."

She looked away and sniffed. "It's very sweet of you to say."

"It's all true. Now, are we here to make him jealous?"

She shrugged.

"Are you willing for people to see you on my arm, for them to think I could be your lover, your man?"

She shrugged once more.

"It's not bad you want him to pay, sweetheart. It's natural, normal."

"He cheated on me with her for six months. She had only turned eighteen when it happened. I know I'm not young, skinny, or beautiful—"

"I'll stop you there, darlin'. Never put yourself down. You're mature, have something men would love to hold on to while they fuck you hard, and are stunning. Not everyone likes young bimbos."

Her chest rose and fell rapidly.

"In fact, I'm not the only man admiring you tonight. If you opened your eyes and saw through the pain, you'll find I'm telling the truth."

Her eyes widened, and slowly she glanced around. I hadn't been lying about anything I'd said. I hoped she saw it when her gaze crossed over the five men looking at her, a couple even raised their drinks her way. Our own beverages arrived, and I told the waitress we needed a moment longer.

When I looked back to Fiona, she was already gazing at me. "You are very good for my confidence."

I winked. "Always happy to help, but you have to remember, I'm one for the truth." I took a sip of my beer. "Now, how about we have some fun? Enjoy each other's company and the meal?"

"That sounds wonderful."

Fiona managed to keep her mind off her ex and have fun talking and laughing until he decided to step up to our table.

"Fiona, what are you doing here?" the dickhead asked harshly.

I stood. "Excuse me, who do you think you are speaking to Fiona that way?"

"I'm her ex-husband."

I looked him over slowly and smirked. "Seriously?"

"Yes," he ground out.

"Nice of you to stop by and say hello, but we were having a nice time, and I don't want you to tarnish it. Please leave."

"Fiona—"

"Leave, Lionel."

He spluttered and stared down at her. Maybe she'd never spoken to him that way before, and if that was the case, I was glad to witness it.

He turned and walked off. I sat back down and smiled widely. "Good job, darlin'."

She grinned back and shrugged. "I guess having you around gave me confidence."

"I'm glad."

As far as first clients went, I was happy with how mine turned out. I dropped Fiona home with a kiss to her cheek and a smile on her face. She was a sweet woman and deserved so much after what her ex had put her through. The poor woman felt unlovable or unworthy. With our time together, I hoped she felt better about herself.

If all clients were like Fiona, I'd be honest-to-God proud of the job I did.

Unfortunately, my smile faded when I remembered I had to head back to Polished to get paid and let Saint know how everything went.

I had to see Saint.

Great.

No doubt I would leave work with a hard-on I would have to take care of myself.

"Jesus motherfuckin' Christ," I swore, which helped me feel more normal. It was okay to put on airs and graces for a short while, but wearing this suit just wasn't me, and I couldn't wait to get back in jeans and a T-shirt.

CHAPTER FOUR
SAINT

There was a quick rap on the door. I didn't get to answer before it was opened. Torch stepped in, along with Kylo. They both seemed in good spirits, laughing about something.

"Hey, brother," Torch called.

"Boss," Kylo said with a nod.

Down, boy, I said to my dick when it perked up like the Scooby-Doo gang did with a clue.

"How did it go tonight?" I asked, leaning my forearms on the desk.

Torch put the camera and mic on the desk. "It was good, fuckin' proud of the little punk. Never heard him speak all proper like that before, but this shithead can put on the charm."

I caught Kylo tense.

Sighing, I scratched at my chin and asked, "Torch, you did tell him the pin has a camera and mic, right?"

Torch grinned. "Nope."

"What do you mean camera?" Kylo clipped.

"Torch was supposed to tell you this pin isn't only a silent alarm, but a camera and mic. The women use it for extra protection. They turn it off when things get down and dirty or don't use it at all except for the alarm."

"Tell me why you didn't explain that?" Kylo demanded.

Torch rolled his eyes. "Come on, don't get your panties in a twist. Knew it was only a date and not anythin' else. I just wanted to see how you went." He turned back to me. "You've got a good one here." He slapped Kylo on the arm. "I'm out. Text me when my next job is." Torch was out the door in seconds.

Shaking my head, I looked at Kylo. "Come here and I'll show you where to switch the camera and mic off." He stepped closer and glanced down at the device. I flipped it over and pointed out the part. "See that? Flick it down, and it'll turn it off. You press the red button if you have an issue and need help. Got it?"

"Yep." He nodded. He still looked a little annoyed at Torch for recording him. I'd be the same, but I was a selfish ass, and I couldn't help but itch to watch that file, which would be sitting on my computer. I wanted to see how Kylo acted, wanted to know what happened. I wanted to know everything.

Why?

I hadn't watched them before unless there had been an issue and our employee wanted us to see what happened.

"Glad it went well tonight. I'll call you when you get the next one. Your money is already transferred into your account." Now he had to get the fuck outta here before I could ask if he'd suck my dick again.

Bee, a sometimes hookup, hadn't done a good job the other night. It hadn't felt as epic as Kylo had done, and I fucking loved getting good head. Maybe it had something to do with the condom I wore with her.

"Thanks," he said and still stood there.

"What's up?"

He jolted. "Sorry?"

I smirked. "Was the date that good you can't stop thinkin' about it?"

"Something like that," he replied with a laugh, but it wasn't a normal one for him. "Do you roughly know when I'll next be on?"

"No, not until it comes up."

"Right." He nodded.

"Okay," I said.

He nodded once more and walked to the door.

Stop! Come back. Get to your knees and fuckin' pleasure me. By the way, you're an asshole for getting my dick addicted to your mouth.

I wondered if he would want my dick in his mouth again. It'd be so fucking wrong to ask, and very damn greedy.

Could I be greedy?

"Kylo," I called as his hand touched the doorknob that I wished was my knob.

Fucking hell.

"Yeah?" he asked, looking over his shoulder.

Open your fucking mouth and just ask. It wouldn't be weird. Who was I kidding? It'd be beyond weird.

I shook my head. "Nothin', have a good night."

He shook his head and turned. "No, you were going to say somethin'. What was it?"

Fuck.

I shrugged. "Can't remember."

He stared at me, crossing his arms over his chest. "Bullshit," he stated.

Prick.

I glared. "It's fuckin' not."

He cocked a brow.

I'd never really looked at him before. He wasn't bad looking for a guy. Young, but I knew he was twenty-three. All right, Jesus Christ, I'd admit he was damn good-looking in his suit. Even in his normal gear. His dark hair was opposite to my blond, but his was shaved at the sides, longer on top. His blue eyes were like a fucking clear blue sky....

What the fuck was I thinking?

"Go get changed and get outta here," I told him. I wasn't giving in to my desire for his mouth.

His jaw clenched. There was no doubt in my mind he wanted to argue some more, and I kind of did too because it was making me hard, and if it came down to it, I would win. But hell, arguing with him would lead to me asking for his mouth.

I wasn't doing it.

As soon as he was out of here, I could leave since Country was taking over for the night. Then I could call a hookup, meet her someplace, and get head.

Would it be as good as Kylo?

I didn't know, but I fucking prayed it would be.

Jenny had a good mouth on her. It'd been a while since I'd used her, and at least she knew it'd be just a one-night thing. She wasn't looking for anything serious.

I grabbed my phone to do just that when Kylo asked, "What were you thinkin'?"

"Nothin', now get outta here so I can go. Country will be here to take over soon." I opened up the chat with Jenny and started to type something out.

"You're callin' a hookup?" Kylo asked, his voice hard.

I jolted and turned in the chair to where he stood close, looking over my shoulder. "What the fuck you think you're doin'?" I clipped.

"You're callin' for some chick to suck your dick," he said again with a glare.

"Among other things, so fuckin' what?" I demanded. "You got no right to look at my personal shit in the first fuckin' place."

"I'll do it," he stated. Then he paled a little and stepped back until he was at the end of the desk.

"Do what?" I asked. My dick and heart already knew what he was getting at. They were both perking up, but my mind wanted clarification.

His hands fisted at his sides. "Don't be a prick. You know what."

I stood, pocketing my wallet and keys. "You want to suck me off?"

"Yes," he hissed, still glaring at me.

I shrugged. "Fine."

"Right then."

"Yep." I nodded, then added, "But not here."

"Agreed."

"Good."

"So where?" he asked.

Shit, where did we go? Lucas was no doubt back at my place with Wreck. The compound was out, too many brothers there. Kylo lived with Boom and Wendy, so that was a no go. From the way Kylo was frowning, it looked like he'd come to the same conclusion.

"There ain't anywhere," I said, making my way to the door. "Looks like it'll have to be Jenny."

"Hold the fuck on," Kylo snarled. Before I faced him, I wiped the smirk off my face. Yeah, he wanted this as much as my dick did.

"What?" I asked.

"Boom and Wendy are stayin' at the compound tonight."

There we have it. He found a solution and was willing to take me back to his place. "I'll follow you," I told him and opened the door wide before stepping to the side. As he passed, I could see the rapid rise and fall of his chest. Was he excited, nervous, or both?

Hell, I knew my dick was thrilled, because I was as hard as steel. My gut was also singing a song of happiness, while my heart swayed to my gut's music.

This was weird, messed up, but fucking thrilling.

I wasn't even going to try and make sense of it. All I had to remember was, bottom line, I was gonna get off.

Boom and Wendy's place was a nice one-story clapboard four-bedroom home. I'd been here when Boom had hosted a cookout, so

I knew it was homey—just like my parents' place had been before they sold it and moved to Australia, only to come back because they'd missed home so much and were now building a smaller place while staying at my aunt's.

As I climbed off my ride, which I'd parked just behind Kylo's, my dick throbbed and my pulse kicked into the next gear. Yeah, I could admit I was nervous, but it was a good kind.

I shoved the negative thoughts of how crazy it was that I was excited about getting head from a *guy* and reminded myself how epic it had been the first time.

I removed my helmet and brought it with me. The area was a good one, but I still didn't trust leaving my shit lying around. Hell, I didn't trust my own area either. Only mine was worse than here.

Stepping up behind Kylo at the front door, I watched as he unlocked it. His hand shook a little. Why did I like seeing that? I liked he was nervous. He even seemed worse than I was.

He opened the door and stepped in, moving to the side. I entered and waited for him to close the front door.

What did we do from here?

Would we do it in the living room? The bathroom? His bedroom?

"In here," he said, opening the first door to the right and turning on the light. I went in and found out it was his bedroom. Surprisingly, it was clean, and I wondered if he did it himself or if Wendy had control over the room.

I walked over to the bed and then turned back to him. He rubbed the back of his neck and glanced around at everything but me. He swallowed. "Yeah, so, I'm just gonna have a quick shower."

"Sure." I nodded.

He waved a hand around. "Make yourself at home."

I chuckled at his actions. Usually he was cocky and self-assured. At least when I laughed, it brought his eyes up to me, and he glared.

He shook his head, walked around the bed, grabbed some

boxers, and left the room. He closed the door a little hard, but hell, I was still smiling.

Why was me messing with him getting me off?

I shrugged at the idea, putting it in the back of my mind. Instead, I took a look around the good-sized room. The walls were dark, and the carpet cream. Two big windows to the right would bring in the sunlight throughout the day and brighten the place nicely. The queen-sized bed sat in the middle of the room, but up against the far wall, and at the end of it was a chaise lounge where, I guessed, Kylo would sit to put his shoes on. There was a bedside table on each side of the bed, and under the bed was a red rug. There was another door in the left corner, which would probably lead to a closet since Kylo walked out of the room to go to the bathroom. Mounted on the wall opposite the bed was a huge TV. Damn, this place was sweet to kick back and relax in after a hard day. Shit, it made me want to redo my bedroom up.

I made my way over to the bedside table. I wanted to search around, figure Kylo out. Maybe there was a clue to how he gave good head, but was I seriously thinking of going through his things?

Yes. Yes, I was.

I never said to anyone I was a good guy.

I pulled open the drawer and found a flashlight, reading glasses, and some pieces of paper. Boring, in other words.

Bending lower, I opened the bottom drawer and stilled.

Holy motherfucking shit. I'd hit the jackpot.

There were condoms, lube, and a goddamn dildo.

What the fuck.

Did he use it on himself? Did he like ass play? I snorted at myself. Of course he liked it; he was into women *and* guys.

Reaching in, I picked it up from the end I knew hadn't been in his ass. Though, no doubt Kylo would clean his stuff down. His room was tidy, after all. The dildo was long, about the size of an average dick, and it weighed a bit.

As the door opened, I straightened and turned, holding up the dildo. Kylo stopped in the doorway, wearing only boxers. His smaller, but built, frame looked good. His face had heated like I'd never seen before, all the way down his neck and the top of his chest. Kylo opened his mouth and snapped, "What the fuck are you doin'?"

"You use this?" I asked.

"Put it the fuck back," he demanded and stormed up to me, grabbing it out of my hand.

"*How* do you use it?" I asked.

He paused, glared at me, and then threw the dildo back in the drawer before kicking it closed. He turned and walked away. He spun back, threw an arm out, opened his mouth, and snapped it closed to grind his teeth together. I smirked, and he narrowed his eyes again.

Kylo blew out a breath and growled his question. "Why were you goin' through my things?"

"Come on. You didn't expect me not to, right?"

"Yes, I did."

I shrugged.

His nostrils flared. "Take your pants off and sit on the damn bed."

My cock jerked. I quirked a brow but went to work on my pants, the button first, then the zipper. I stopped there and took off my vest as I walked toward him, where he stood at the end of the bed. I put my vest over the side of the chaise lounge and removed my tee.

Kylo sucked in harshly. "What are you doin'?"

"If you can't guess, I guess I'll tell you. Takin' off my clothes."

"Why?" he whispered.

"Did you offer to suck my dick?"

He blinked. "Well, yes, but—"

"So I'm gettin' ready."

"You could have just undone your pants, and that's it," he stated.

I chuckled. He was uncomfortable seeing me naked. Good. I grinned and kicked off my boots, took off my socks, and pushed down my jeans along with my boxers, also kicking them off. I looked to Kylo, and as his gaze ran over me, he breathed heavily.

"Fuck," he muttered.

Walking around him, I went to the other side of the bed and sat down, leaning my back against the wall. Kylo stared down at me like I'd lost my mind. Maybe I had, but this shit was fun.

"Do you want a drink? I need a drink. We should have a drink. Beer? Whiskey?" He shook his head but didn't look away from my hard dick.

"Sure, I'll take a whiskey, straight."

He nodded but didn't move, besides his hands fisting and unfisting at his sides. Was he trying to stop himself from coming at me? From grabbing me?

"Kylo," I called. He snapped his gaze up to me. "Drink?"

"Right. Yeah. Okay." He nodded and then walked from the room.

I didn't care that being there waiting for his mouth was something out of my normal. I was having the time of my life making Kylo sweat. I also felt like my head grew a few inches from the way he eyed me like I was candy.

I couldn't wait to be eaten.

CHAPTER FIVE
KYLO

"Holy fuckin' Christ, what's he doin' to me?" I muttered to myself as I went to get us drinks. I was getting a naked Saint a drink while he sat his bare ass on my bed. He was in my room, on my bed, waiting for me. Naked.

I couldn't make sense of it. My mind was running too fast. I didn't know what to think. But fuck it. I was getting a drink for us and then would go back in there and blow him.

"He's naked in there," I told myself, and still, it was like a wet dream come true. Was I imagining this? Was I dreaming?

His fucking body was a wet dream. All muscles were on display, and I'd looked. Boy, did I look. Long and hard. It was why I had to get out of there for a breather before I came in my boxers without actually any action.

This shit was crazy.

But a good kind.

My body felt like it'd been pumped full of adrenaline and Viagra. My dick had never been so hard… well, except for the time I sucked him off in the office.

He was here.

He was here because I'd offered to give him a blow job again. I could hit myself for saying something in the first place. However, he'd been the one to start it when he'd looked like he was going to ask for one but then didn't.

I couldn't back down. I couldn't walk away, not after I saw the text he had ready for that fucking hookup. All I could think was that if he was going to get off from anyone, it would be me.

Again, I was crazy.

I fixed the drinks and took them back into the bedroom. He still sat on my bed naked. I hadn't been dreaming, only now he had his phone out and had been flicking through it until I stepped back into the room. He put it down when I walked toward him, holding out his drink.

"Thanks," he said, and then took a sip where I threw mine back and put the empty glass down on the bedside table. I glanced back down at him to find him smirking. Only his eyes were on my erection tenting my boxers.

He ran his eyes up my body, and I felt extra hot from the action. When he caught my gaze, he smiled.

Smiled like he wanted this, like he didn't care I was a guy about to suck him.

Did he ever get flustered?

The bastard.

He winked, and I wanted to punch him but kiss him also. Damn him and his unshakeable attitude. He gestured to his still hard cock with his eyes and then back up to me.

I went to bend down, but he shook his head and spread his legs.

Fucking hell.

He wanted me between his legs.

I swallowed hard and then slowly climbed on the bed between his legs. Christ, he looked good on my bed, waiting for me. He winked again and then took another sip of his drink before resting it on the bed in his hand.

Reaching out, I ran my hands up his thighs, surprised to see him shiver. He actually wanted this.

Wanted me.

The knowledge blew me out of the fucking water.

I dipped down, kissed the tip of his dick, and ran my tongue down the outer edge and then back up before gripping the base of his erection and holding it out to myself. I grinned, excited to have him in my mouth again.

I licked around the tip and glanced up to find him watching me, even as he drank from his glass.

Christ, he was hot.

I took him in deep, keeping his gaze, witnessing his eyes heating. "Fuck yeah," he murmured. I slid my mouth back up and then down again. I removed one hand from gripping his hip and cupped his balls, rolling them gently in my hand.

"Jesus," he hissed.

I froze when his hand—his fucking hand—reached out to me. *To me*. He threaded his fingers through the top of my hair and tugged. I moaned around his cock, and he hissed out a breath. I bobbed up and down faster, thrilled he wanted to touch me while I sucked him.

Fuck, I wanted to reach down and rub myself until I came, but he'd probably freak out over it. He could think it was too much. Too real. I wouldn't risk it even though my body craved its own release.

His balls drew up, and I sucked him over and over. I drew them down with my fingers. His hand tightened even more on my hair, but he let me go at my own pace, didn't force his dick into my mouth, and I was glad for it because I would come then. I liked it a little rough. I liked to gag and be told what to do.

"Kylo, fuck," he shouted just before the first drop shot into my mouth. He ground up and released the rest of his load. I took it all, right until the last drop I dragged out of the end with my hand.

He'd never be mine like the way I wanted.

He'd never dominate me.

Fuck.

Why did I have to realize it now?

I sat back on my knees and caught his smile before he took the last sip of his drink. I looked away and went to get off the bed, but my wrist was caught. I didn't even get to glance back before I was pulled down next to him.

My eyes widened; my pulse raced when he shifted down the bed to lie next to me.

I wanted to ask what he was doing but was afraid if I voiced it, I'd stuff up the words and look like a fucking fool.

Saint hummed under his breath. He looked down at me as he rested his hand on my fast rising and falling chest.

"You were right," he said in a deep, lazy voice.

"Huh?" I managed and then froze when his hand glided down from my chest, down over my stomach, which fucking fluttered, before he pushed it under my boxers and took hold of my aching dick.

"Kylo?"

"Huh?" I mumbled, staring down and silently begging for him to move his hand over me.

"I said you were right. Want to know what about?"

I nodded.

"Na-uh, you gotta use words. Say, 'yes, Saint, I want to know what I'm right about.'"

Just move your hand, motherfucker.

Licking my suddenly dry lips, I said, "Yes, Saint, I want to know what I'm right about."

"Good, Kylo," he breathed, his nose rubbing up and down the side of my face. "You were right. You have skills to make me come in minutes."

I nodded. *Move your hand. Please.*

"But do you want to know something else?"

No. Yes... maybe. I nodded.

"I can make you come in minutes as well." His hand then ran up and down my length under my boxers. It was slow to start with and then faster. I closed my eyes, arched my back, lifted my legs, bending them and thrusting up and down into his grip.

"Open your eyes, Kylo," Saint ordered. I did, and he smiled down at me. "Feel good?" he asked. I nodded. "You close?" I nodded again. He grinned again.

"Saint," I whispered.

"Yeah, right here. Got your dick in my hand, Kylo. Fuck it… yeah, just like that. Hell, you move like you were made to. Look at you, fucking my hand. You like that, Kylo?"

I groaned out, "Yes," and then shot my load into my boxers and over Saint's hand. His hand stopped pumping me, though he gave one last tug, which had me shuddering.

Then it registered I just came in my boxers by Saint's hand.

Holy, holy fuck.

I sat up. "Right, I'll… yeah, be back." I scooted off the bed like a damn idiot and walked out of the room. I was sure I heard chuckling behind me, but my ears were ringing. My heart was thumping, and I was running from the room because all of a sudden, knowing Saint jacked me off was too much. I went into the living room and paced. I ran a hand through my hair a couple of times and then stopped, putting my hands on my hips.

Saint jacked me off.

He'd had his hand around my dick.

Again, it was like he didn't even care I was a guy.

We'd known each other a while, and suddenly, he was touching my dick like he hadn't a care about the change at all.

Why was I freaking out over this? Shit, I didn't need to worry; it was a good thing for me, right? Probably fucking not because I'd get attached to the guy. This was just a quick play with me. He would never be interested in a damn relationship.

Not that I wanted one.

I didn't.

At least, I didn't think I did.

Fuck.

Fuck.

Right, this was easy. I would have to stay away from him, so I didn't get attached. I'd keep away. I'd have to because he was just messing around for a while before he found the one woman he wanted to settle down with.

Not that I was thinking of a relationship with *him*. I wasn't. Hell, I could settle down with an old lady and not a guy in the end. Depended on who I fell in love with. I wasn't holding onto something with Saint that would pass for him like it was nothing.

I nodded to myself. I grabbed a clean pair of boxers out of the laundry basket on the couch and went into the bathroom. I cleaned myself up with a washcloth, dried, and put on the clean pair before grabbing a cloth for Saint.

Shaking out my arms, I went back into the bedroom and tossed the cloth to Saint. He caught it, having been watching the door with a smile. He wiped down his hands while watching me as I walked around the other side of the bed and picked up his clothes. I put them at the end of the bed near his feet and then walked back around. Climbing on the bed, I leaned back against the wall and grabbed the remote. I switched on the TV and waited. I could feel his eyes on me and just knew he was smirking. He always smirked. I took a quick glance his way and found he was, before changing the channel.

Saint stood, stretched, and looked over, catching me watching him. I refocused on the TV. He chuckled. "Want another drink?" he asked.

What the fuck? He should have been running for the damn door. Wasn't that his style after a hookup?

"Sure," I drew out.

He leaned forward, picked up his boxers, and put them on before he grabbed our glasses and left the room. He was staying. He was going to get us a drink. Did he even know where the bar was?

He wasn't making sense.

Maybe if I pretended to be asleep before he got back, he'd leave.

That was a stupid idea; it'd also look weird.

Before I could do anything, Saint was back in the room with a drink in each hand. Of course he was still smirking. Jesus, I wanted to yell at him to quit it. He handed one to me and then sat back on the bed. I watched him take a sip of his drink before eyeing the TV.

This was stranger than the sucking-off situation.

"Kylo," he said, his tone neutral.

"Yeah?" I asked and looked at him.

"Why the fuck are we watching this kids' show?"

I swung my gaze back to the TV, and it penetrated what I'd left it on. Some fucked-up costumed things that didn't even talk.

"This just came on. Somethin' else was on first," I said and changed the channel. I stopped on a basketball game. We stayed silent and watched it for a bit while sipping our drinks.

It wasn't bad just chilling in my room with Saint… except for the fact I'd just sucked his dick again and he'd made me come—hard—and I couldn't stop thinking about it, but I needed to because we couldn't make it a regular thing. Saint would soon understand just what he'd been doing, and then he'd be a normal straight guy and freak out before getting out of there. Then it'd be awkward between us at work and the compound. Great.

Saint put his glass on the bedside table and got off the bed. He went to his clothes and started to dress, all while watching me. I felt his gaze burning into me even though I kept mine on the TV. Finally, he was acting normal.

"Kylo," he called. I looked to him as he walked back to where he'd left his phone. Then he had my eyes again. He put a knee to the bed, leaned over, and pressed his lips to my shoulder.

"Night," he said, and looked up at me.

I cleared my thick throat.

He'd kissed my shoulder.

My skin.

"Yeah, night." I nodded. He grinned, straightened, and walked from the room.

What the hell was that all about?

Why did he do that?

This was fucking weird. Saint made no sense. I scrubbed a hand over my face.

I hadn't expected the first time he'd agreed for me to give him head, but then it happened a second time, and he'd had his hand in my boxers, wrapped around my dick. Then he kissed my shoulder.

That was intimate.

Right, I was going to have to get him out of my head, away from my body, and when I had to, we'd speak like boss and employee.

His ride started up out the front. I went to leap off the bed but locked my body down. It was strange that I suddenly thought that I didn't want him to go. I shook my head. I did want him to go. I did. He had to.

I groaned and shook my head. I got off the bed and went to have another shower. I'd push him in the back of my mind and concentrate on work, both at the compound and for Polished.

I would have believed myself more if I didn't masturbate in the damn shower over the vision of Saint jacking me off. Only that time, he would dip his head and kiss me like he wanted to make me his. I would have believed myself if I hadn't cried his name at the end.

Fuck me. It was going to be hard being around him and trying to forget what just happened between us.

He'd *kissed* my shoulder.

He was acting so damn weird.

And it sucked that I kind of liked it. I wished I didn't.

Fuck me. I was screwed.

CHAPTER SIX
SAINT

month after going back to Kylo's, I walked into the compound common room whistling. The other nights I'd been here, Kylo hadn't been working the bar. That night, I knew he was, and I needed my fix of seeing him. I wasn't stupid; he'd been dodging me because no doubt he was worried about my actions. What helped him keep his distance was that I'd been a fuckton busy. Hell, I hadn't even gotten laid in ages. Still, I'd been in a good mood ever since that night because it'd been damn fun to see Kylo squirm with his thoughts, actions and, maybe, feelings. I could tell he thought I was going to run from the room after making him come in his boxers and over my hand. Then, when I didn't, he didn't know how to act or what to say.

It goddamn entertained me so much.

I also enjoyed just sitting there with him, having a drink. It didn't matter we didn't talk. I liked being around him. And since that time in his bedroom, he kept popping up in my thoughts. Hell, it was making me feel good, so I was going to run with it. I was sure Kylo didn't mind finding release, even by my hand; he'd probably want to do it again.

I hoped.

"Hey, Saint." Death waved me over from the bar. I headed that way and greeted other brothers when they called out to me. My smile ticked up even more when I saw Kylo behind the bar. However, he hadn't moved since Death called out my name. He was looking down at something and standing still. We'd seen each other every week at work, but I'd always had someone else in the office when he'd come in, which was why I was there that night. So I could pay better attention to him. That and catching up with the brothers.

Then Torch called him from the other end of the bar and Kylo jerked into action, heading down there to get him a drink.

I clasped Death on the shoulder and said, "What's happenin', brother?"

"Same old." He lifted a chin Kylo's way. "Still can't believe the prospect's action on the file. Said it before, but I'll say it again, that kid has skills."

I grinned. He sure did have skills, only I was thinking of different ones. I'd also watched the video quite a few times, in fact. "Agreed, he sure can butter someone up sweetly. That client's asked for him twice more and put her friends onto him as well."

Death chuckled. "Great for business."

"Hell yes, all the new employees have done well." I sat down on the stool next to him just as Bethy arrived at my side. She curled her arm around my shoulders and kissed my cheek. I heard something smash at the other end of the bar and glanced over. Kylo was burning red as he started picking some glass up from the floor.

"What's up with him?" I asked Death, even though I knew it was from my entrance. Shit, it was funny and sweet at the same time.

Death shrugged. "Accident?"

"Probably."

Death yelled, "Comes outta your pay, prospect."

Kylo waved him off, taking note, but got back to work getting another drink.

Bethy's other hand slid to my stomach. I caught her eyes and grabbed her hand. "Not now, honey."

She pouted. "But, baby…."

I winked. "Maybe later, yeah. If you haven't got another brother goin', that is."

She giggled. "We'll have to wait and see." She kissed my cheek and walked off, swaying her hips.

Bethy, like most women here, were club sluts. They were at the compound to party and fuck, and that was it. Okay, there were some who wanted to find an old man in the brotherhood, but we were smart enough not to join ourselves with a club slut because all they were after was the biker life. Not something real.

It was good to have them around when we wanted a wet hole to sink into, but I wasn't into a relationship with a woman who had fucked all the other single, and some married, brothers.

"Not feelin' it tonight?" Death asked when she was out of earshot.

"Nah, brother. Well, not Bethy anyway." I didn't dare look down the bar at Kylo because Death picked up on a lot of shit before it even registered in the person actually doing it. But yeah, I was in the mood for Kylo's mouth once again. It'd been too damn long, and while the game of Kylo avoiding me was fun, I wanted to be around him more. I was ready to chase. Christ, my dick was so eager it jerked in my pants as if in search of my desires. Smiling, I asked, "What about you?" to get my mind off him.

He snorted. "Brother, you know I don't go near the bunnies around here."

Yeah, I did, but my mind had been on someone, and I'd forgot for a moment. Death preferred his women away from the compound. His tastes were flight attendants, bankers, lawyers, hell, anything that could challenge him and not be an easy piece of ass.

"Yeah, I remember."

"Who's at the club tonight?"

"State."

"Did you hear about what happened to him a couple of days ago?" Death asked.

I nodded. "Yeah, fuckin' stupid pigs." State had been out on a date with the woman he was chasing, and the cops busted it up by arresting him on a charge of murder, which was all crap. It was lucky we had a good lawyer on the payroll. However, we hadn't needed to call our lawyer since State's woman had got one of the best in town, with the help of her parents, and sent them quickly to attend State. I could see good things happening for State and Courtney.

Kylo stopped in front of us. He gave us a chin lift. "Get you two anythin'?"

"Another beer," Death said.

"I'll have a whiskey." I grinned.

He paused for a beat and then got to getting our drinks. Yeah, he was thinking about what happened in his bedroom—didn't matter that a month had passed. Would he be hard? Had he enjoyed it as much as I did? Or was he still in his freak-out mode where whatever I did was throwing him off his usual game?

As he got our drinks, I turned to Death and asked him, "How's business goin'?"

"Busy, always fuckin' busy. We're a bit run off our feet after openin' the new brothels as well as another butcher shop."

"Thought there'd be enough brothers with experience to help out?"

"Yeah, but I might eventually look into more, but then again, there's more work involved with trainin' them up." He grabbed the beer Kylo held out. Death went on talking about something, but I watched as Kylo placed my drink down on the bar. Before he could move his hand away, I reached out and ran my fingers over his. I caught his jolt out of the corner of my eyes and felt him pull his hand away quickly as I nodded to Death.

"Maybe we should look at sellin' the butcher places, and we'd have more brothers for the security side of things. Be better than employin' outsiders."

Death thought for a moment, then shrugged. "Somethin' to think about."

I nodded and sensed Kylo move back down the bar.

"Saint" was cooed from my other side. I turned and found Lee, another club girl. She ran her hand over my back. "How you doin', baby?"

"Real good, darlin', but busy talkin' with my brother." I smacked her on the ass. "Might catch ya later."

She smiled sultrily. "You got it." Then she walked away, knowing not to approach Death since he'd set all the women straight at the beginning. If we got new girls, he'd tell them the same thing—he wasn't interested.

Me? I wasn't in the mood to taste female that night. I had an urge for one person only, and he was doing everything he could to avoid me. That'd change by the end of the night.

I wasn't being cocky. He wouldn't have offered to suck me off if he wasn't interested in me, even in a small way. He just didn't know how to take me and my sudden change. Fuck, I didn't know how to take myself, but I was going along with it because I enjoyed the way Kylo could make me feel. Christ, I hadn't felt giddy in the gut in a fucking long time.

Maybe it was the thrill of the secret or trying something new… but I reckoned it had something to do with the man himself. Thinking back, when he'd first started tagging along with Boom, before he became a prospect, I'd enjoyed listening to him and watching him because I could never anticipate what he'd do or say. He was open, like the shit he'd blurted about liking Lucas, my brother. It was also the time that Wreck had him against the wall for saying something stupid.

Wait, did he just do shit with me because of Lucas? My brother and I didn't look much alike. I was more like our old man, taller, wider, gruffer than our sweet and short mother, except for the blond hair.

Christ, I wasn't thinking of that now. I wasn't comparing or competing against Lucas, not when Kylo knew Lucas was out of the picture because of Wreck. Hell, if he still had a thing for Lucas, it'd be stupid. Kylo knew Wreck would kick his ass.

I didn't want to think. I didn't want to worry. I just wanted to enjoy, and I fucking would because I was a greedy prick.

Some other brothers joined Death and me, and we talked about random shit—our rides, traveling, business, the club. I'd always loved to come to the compound to catch up with everyone. There were some brothers I didn't care for, but hell, our club was big, and I didn't have to face them most of the time.

Like Duck. He'd been a member until he'd gone against Lucas and Wreck the night Lucas had been here as Wreck's guy for the first time. Not all could respect the connection Lucas and Wreck had—some found it disgusting and wrong. Duck was stupid enough to voice his repulsion, and he paid for it. Country, our club president, didn't like bigotry of any kind. He kicked Duck out, and it showed the other brothers what not to do when it came to the members loving who they wanted.

I'd always known my brother was gay, not that he'd told us until recently, but it didn't matter to me. He was Lucas, and there was nothing wrong with my brother because he loved a man. Hell, I'd never admit it to them, but I was damn happy to see them all loved up and lost in each other. In a way, I was jealous. I wanted that for me, just not yet.

I liked having fun and playing, but one day I'd settle down. Only I wasn't sure if it'd be with a woman or a man now. My head and heart hadn't worked out what I preferred just yet since I'd only gotten a taste of having a guy.

It was strange I'd switched up. That I'd even be thinking of a guy in my life, and it'd happened after one blow job from Kylo. But I'd go with it. There was no denying the way I craved more from him.

I'd been picturing taking his mouth in a hard and hot kiss. Though, I wanted more from Kylo than just his mouth.

While the others were talking, I glanced down the other end where Kylo was. I tensed, locked my jaw, and narrowed my eyes.

He was leaning into the bar with his elbows resting on top of it, laughing at something Dusty said. She was another club girl, a newer one, and a favorite to flirt with because she was shy and didn't just sleep with anyone. She was pickier about who she went to bed with, and we'd let her be since she was also young. Only nineteen. As far as I knew, she'd only been with Country a couple of times when he got rid of Isla, since he found her making out with another member.

I didn't like seeing her with Kylo, though.

A ripple of surprise spread through me, and I smiled. Yeah, I was into the guy, and it took me getting head to wake me up to the possibility of him.

Only the smile dropped when Dusty reached out and tapped her fist into his arm with a playful punch and a cute smile. Kylo grinned and winked before saying something that had Dusty blushing.

I looked away and checked out some other brothers—thinking if Kylo could get me hard from looking at him, maybe some other guy would as well.

Nothing happened though.

I'd admit there were a lot of good-looking brothers, but none of them got my pulse racing like Kylo did when I pictured just his face and body.

When I heard laughter again from the other end, I got up off my stool and strode down that way.

"Whiskey, prospect," I ordered roughly and stopped by Dusty. Kylo nodded and got my drink. I turned to Dusty and smiled. Only it mustn't have been a good one because her brows dipped. "Hey, girl. Can you give us a second?"

"Uh, sure, of course, Saint."

"Thanks, babycakes." I winked. Dusty gave me one last unsure gaze before scooting off somewhere.

A glass dropped to the bar, whiskey sloshed over the edges, but I just grinned and picked it up, taking a sip. Kylo glared and went to walk off, but I said, "Here. Now, Kylo," I demanded roughly but quietly.

He froze, then came unstuck and turned back to me.

I twisted the glass on the counter while I watched him. When I didn't say anything, he made a noise of annoyance in the back of his throat. I smirked. "How you been?"

He ground his teeth. "Good."

"Been wonderin', how come you never prospected in until you were twenty-two?"

He studied me for a moment before saying, "Boom wanted me to be completely sure this was what I wanted. Even when I'd told him it was, he got me to hold off for a bit longer. I think it was also for Wendy's sake, so she could get used to it. She's always worried about the shit we deal with from the cops and other clubs."

"She's a good woman."

He nodded. "Yeah, she is."

I hummed under my breath, and just to have a conversation, I asked, "We haven't had a chat about work. Been busy. Just wanted to know how it's goin'?" I'd been keeping him with older women who were just after some eye candy to show off for the night. Kylo was eye candy, and the women were lapping him up and asking for more.

He shrugged. "Nothin' new, but you know that."

"You helpin' Lucas and Wreck tomorrow to move in?" I asked instead.

"Yeah." His brows dinted in the middle. "All of this you could have said in front of Dusty. Why'd you send her away?"

It was my turn to shrug. "Didn't want her around."

He scoffed. "You didn't mind the other two around you."

I grinned like a cat who got the cream. He'd been jealous. He went back to glaring. I took a sip before saying, "They were just bein' friendly and greetin' me."

He rolled his eyes. "Sure. And that's why I heard you sayin' you'd catch them later."

When I ran my tongue over my bottom lip, I saw his eyes following. "You jealous, Kylo?"

He sucked in a sharp breath and then forced a laugh. "What the fuck! No."

A cloth appeared, and he scrubbed the counter down, keeping his eyes on his job. From the slight flush, I knew I flustered him. Good. Then, he was lucky—someone called his name, and he turned and bolted. I stayed where I was, wanting to see if he'd drift back to me. I pulled my phone from my pocket and checked it. I had a message sitting there from my mom, Lucy.

Mom: Hello, my precious boy. I have another phone number for you. I'll give it to you tomorrow and tell you about my friend's daughter. But let me just say, she's a sweetheart. I'm sure you'll love her.

Apparently, Mom had a lot of friends' daughters she wanted to set me up with recently. It was fortunate I'd managed to be busy every time she'd tried to get me to call someone. Mom had been all happy since Lucas and Wreck started dating, and she wanted me to settle down and find a good girl.

Me: Mom, I love you, but no.

Mom: Lol, talk to you tomorrow. Love you.

Dad: Boy, just go on one date with one of them for FS. Then your mom will stop harping in my ear.

I groaned.

Me: Dad, I'm not taking one for the team. You married her. You put up with it because I'm not interested at the moment.

Dad: Good luck with her tomorrow then. Then he sent me a GIF of a character laughing hard. The ass.

Shaking my head, I lifted my gaze. "You came back." I grinned.

"What are you doin'?" he asked.

I put a hand to my heart and spoke in a southern accent, at least to me it sounded like one. "Whatever do you mean?"

His lips twitched, but he wouldn't give into laughing. "Saint."

"Yeah?" I asked and took another sip of my drink.

He blinked slowly. "Do you need anythin' else?"

I licked the alcohol off my lips. His eyes fluttered down to watch the action, and my cock gave a jerk. Kylo wanted to kiss me.

Fuck yeah. I'd be on board with that.

"You want a taste?"

He jerked back. "What?" he whispered harshly.

I leaned in, holding the glass between two hands and asked, "Do you wanna taste my mouth?" His eyes widened even more. He went to look around, but I shook my head and ordered, "Just look at me. I'll let you know if anyone comes close."

He opened his mouth, then closed it and threw out a hand. What he didn't do was answer me.

I grinned. "You gonna tell me, Kylo? Do you wanna kiss me?"

He made a noise in the back of his throat. I wasn't sure if it was a yes or a no, though. "You confuse me."

"Good." I could tell he wasn't doing well with people around, worried someone would overhear. I'd have to bring this up at a later date since I wouldn't get anywhere tonight, and really, I needed a decent night's sleep if I had to be up early to help Lucas and Wreck move.

Then I'd have my house back to myself and I could have anyone over.

It'd be a loss not having Kylo tonight, but the wait would be worth it.

I stood, winked, and said, "See you tomorrow." On the way out, I said goodbye to other brothers, and before I walked out, I glanced back to catch Kylo watching me. I shot him a wave. Excitement bubbled the fuck up inside me. I was looking forward to getting an answer from him because I reckoned he definitely wanted a taste of my mouth, and I wanted to give him that. I didn't care I was his boss or that I was fully patched into the club and he wasn't. What I wanted from Kylo had nothing to do with either of those things. When I was around him outside of the business and club, I was just Zion and he was Kylo. I'd never hold anything over him. I just wanted him.

CHAPTER SEVEN
KYLO

*T*he man had lost his mind. Saint had gone crazy and was pulling me down into insane land as well. Before last night, I'd managed to evade him for a while. It'd been mainly based on luck and how busy he was at work, but then he'd come to the compound and completely set my nerves alight to eat my insides. When he looked at me when I heard his voice, when the women approached him, and then, fucking *then* when he'd asked me if I wanted to taste his mouth….

Christ, I'd nearly cried yes, but I'd clamped my mouth closed and probably acted like a fool. I couldn't really remember because I'd been stuck on the words *taste* and *mouth*.

"Earth to Kylo," Quake called. We'd both just arrived to help and stood outside of Lucas and Wreck's new place. I'd been lost in thought already because I knew Saint would be here and I wasn't ready to face him.

Do you wanna taste my mouth?

Shaking that thought away, I asked, "Sorry?"

"You okay, brother?" he asked.

I pushed out a laugh. "Yeah, I'm fine," I told him, and then grabbed my own box from the moving truck and took it inside. I kept myself busy, and every time my mind went to Saint, I thought of something else.

It kind of worked, until I was carrying another box in and I heard Saint in the kitchen saying something about going on a date. The box slipped when I went to lean in more to listen and dropped to the floor. Something smashed inside it. Fucking hell, how could he be talking about a date when he'd asked me about tasting his mouth?

That right there was why I had to keep a distance.

"It's okay," I called, and then peeked around the corner. I kept my eyes on Lucas as I smiled. "Promise, I didn't break it. It was already broken."

Saint snorted and then left the room. Why did he walk out? I was surprised he didn't stay to mess with me some more.

"Kylo, I didn't know you arrived." Lucas smiled. I hadn't hunted Lucas down as yet because I knew he would probably be able to tell something was up.

"Hang the fuck on," Wreck said. "How about we get back to what he broke?"

"He said it was already broken," Lucas put in for me.

Wreck looked down at his man with high brows. "And you believe him?"

"Well, yes?"

I laughed. "You don't sound convincin'." Lucas was never good at lying. I'd been attracted to him when I first met him. He'd been shy and cute, and I wanted to get to know him. I soon recognized we were better as friends than anything, which saved my life no doubt since Wreck had fallen for the guy as well.

"I'm working on my acting skills," Lucas admitted.

Wreck snorted while I smiled again. See, he was just damn charming.

"How's work going?" he asked me and I froze. Work was good. It was the boss that wasn't, but I couldn't tell him that his brother was a big fucking prick who sent me insane.

Thankfully, West, Lucas's other friend, and also mine now, arrived.

However, I shouldn't have been thankful too quickly because Lucas piped up with "I can ask you the same question. How's work going?"

My mind went right to Saint. *Do you wanna taste my mouth?*

I shrugged, answering first with "Same old. Anyway, I better go clean up the mess—not that there is a mess to clean up," I added quickly when Wreck's frosty stare hit me.

I made my way out of there but heard West laugh and then say, "I'm good too, and I'll go help him before your man kills him." West caught up with me as I picked up the box. I winced when things rattled in there.

"Take it out front and we'll check it where Wreck can't hear."

I snorted. "Good thinkin'." We went outside, and West opened the back door to his car so I could place it in there. I opened it and clipped, "Shit."

Looking over my shoulder, West whistled. "He's going to kill you."

I stepped back and closed the door. "Not if he doesn't find it."

West's eyes rounded. "You're not leaving that in there. I presume they were Wreck's."

Nodding, I said, "At the compound, Wreck had his favorite coffee cups. He didn't like anyone touchin' them."

"I know. He had one at Lucas and Saint's place, and he nearly bit my head off for going to use it."

"Fuck."

"Yes." He nodded.

Groaning, I leaned against his car and hoped West would forget they were in there until he pulled away with them. "So, you gonna tell me what's goin' on with you?"

He kicked at the ground. "I don't know what you're talking about."

"Why have you been dodgin' Lucas?"

His hand went to his hips. "Why have you?"

I snorted. "Fair enough, and I'm not now." I waited a beat and then added, "Just, if you need to talk and don't feel like poppin' into their bubble of happiness, I'm here."

He smiled, lifted his leg, and tapped his foot against mine. "Same goes for you."

"What's goin' on?" a new voice said, one I recognized.

Saint stepped around West's car. Where he'd come from, I wasn't sure. Maybe he'd been on his phone setting up a date.

I glared. "What're you doin'?"

He held up his phone. "On a call."

Fucking knew it. Asshole.

"What were you two whisperin' about?" Saint asked as he stopped beside me to lean against West's car.

"Nothing," West said quickly. Too quickly.

Saint's brows rose. He twisted my way more, leaning just his left side into West's car. My gut danced around. Saint laughed. "Oh, now I know I'm onto somethin'. What did you two do, and it better fuckin' not be each other."

I sucked in a sharp breath and then choked on my saliva while West just stood there and stared at Saint like he didn't know him. It was possible he didn't because I wasn't sure of this side of Saint either.

"Why couldn't we do each other?" West stupidly questioned.

Saint swung a scowl at West, who took a step back. West then looked to me, where I shrugged, and then back to Saint, as Saint said, "Because..." I held my breath. Where in the hell would he go with this? "...I'd be pissed. There's a rule that employees can't sleep together."

I relaxed a little. Saint was going to give me a heart attack.

West gave off a shaky laugh. "Not to worry there, Saint. We're not sleeping together."

Saint grinned wide. "Good to know then. So what were you guys hidin' in the back of the car?"

He fucking knew all along we had something in the car, so why question if we were screwing? Jesus Christ, I wanted to punch him, grab him, and kiss him all at once.

"Mugs," West said. "Wreck's mug."

Saint let out a bark of laughter. "Shit, you guys are gonna get it."

"It was Kylo," West said, and caught my glare before he added, "I'm getting back to work." Then he practically ran away to the moving van and grabbed another box.

A hand brushed over my hip and I immediately realized I should have followed him. I jolted, straightened, and stepped forward.

"Kylo," Saint called.

I turned. "Shouldn't you be calling me 'prospect'?"

He shrugged, putting his hands in his pockets and leaning back against the car. "What are you doin' tonight?"

"Busy" was all I said.

He grinned and rocked forward, then moved closer to me. "What're you doin'?"

"Gettin' back to helpin'."

He shook his head. "What are you doin' tonight?"

"Workin'."

He clucked his tongue. "Kylo, I know you're not." His hands linked behind his head as he stretched. His tee and vest rode up, and my eyes clung to his abs and the fucking V that dipped into his black jeans. Saint cleared his throat. I quickly flicked my gaze up to see the satisfied smirk on his mouth.

Motherfucker.

Though it didn't matter that I was attracted to him. I knew not to get involved with a guy who was just testing the bisexual waters.

"Come to my place tonight," he said.

I shook my head. "No."

"Why?"

"Like I said I'm—"

"If you say busy, I'm gonna get pissed. I know you're not. I'll pick you up at seven," he stated and then walked by me.

"Saint—"

"Seven," he ordered.

"Saint—"

He spun back and snapped, "It's Zion, and I swear to fuckin' Christ, if you're not at your place at seven, I'll hunt you down, and it won't be pretty."

I shut my mouth. He eyed me for a beat longer, probably waiting for me to say something, but I was blank. Utterly blank. He then nodded, turned, and stalked off.

What the fuck just happened?

I wasn't going to be home when he arrived. I wasn't. It was fucking foolish to be home waiting to be picked up for God knows what. Admittedly, I kinda did know. He wanted another blow job, but I wouldn't give one. He wasn't getting anything from me. I glanced down at my watch. I had half an hour to get out of there. I would leave… I would.

Yet, there I stood in my room, not moving, when a knock came to the door. My heart pounded as if it wanted to race to the door to answer it.

"Kid," Boom yelled.

It was only Boom…. Fuck, it was Boom. What were they doing home, and how did they get home without my hearing them? "Come in," I called.

He opened the door and stepped in. "Hey."

"Hi," I said a little too high. "I thought you two were headin' to the compound?"

"Had to drop back 'cause Wendy forgot her purse. She's out in the car waitin'." His head tilted as he stared at me. "You all right? I didn't catch you jerkin' off, did I? You're a little panicky and sweaty."

"Fuckin' hell, Boom. No, I wasn't wackin', and please, for the love of our rides, never ask me that again."

He chuckled. "Sure, but so you know there ain't anythin' wrong with—"

"Boom. Stop." I shook my head. "What did you need anyway?"

"Just wanted to double-check you still wanted to stay in and not come."

"Yeah… actually, I might come. I'll just grab my wallet. Meet you out front."

"Got it."

At least then, I could tell Saint that Boom needed me at the compound for some lame reason. Then I wasn't exactly lying. Why was I even thinking of something to tell him? I wasn't supposed to care.

Shaking my head, I grabbed my wallet off the bedside table and walked out of the house, locking it behind me. I turned and froze.

"Kid, look who's here," Boom yelled.

Saint stood next to Boom and Wendy, smiling.

Cunt of a motherfucking whore.

Boom slapped Saint on the back. "He's come to grab your help with some shit, so we'll leave you to it."

"But…," I called loudly and then caught myself. "Didn't you want me to come to the compound?"

Boom laughed. "Don't worry about it. It's good to help a brother out. Come on, Wendy, let's jet."

"Later, boys. Behave yourselves." Wendy waved with a soft smile.

Saint chuckled. "We'll try to, Wendy, but you just never know what we'll get up to."

Wendy giggled. "Oh, you, always a teaser."

Saint winked. I stayed where I was and knew I was out of options to get away from the man. Unless I ran inside and barred myself in there; if only it didn't make me look like a pussy, I would have done that. Instead, I didn't move and waved Wendy and Boom off when they left.

"So," Saint drew out, and I noticed then that he wore just boots, jeans, and a tee. He didn't have his club vest on. I wouldn't get mine until I was a full member, but Saint always wore his. Why wasn't he now? He continued with "You were goin' to the compound?"

"No," I lied, even though Boom just said as much.

Saint laughed. "It was lucky I showed up a bit early." He started for the street where his car was parked. "Well, come on," he called.

"I'm not feelin' the best," I lied once more.

Saint rolled his eyes, walked back to me, and grabbed my hand and pulled me along after him. "Don't know why you're tryin' to get out of this. It'll be fun."

Fun?

Sex… I meant, head jobs were fun?

Well, I supposed they were, but I would have said pleasurable.

He opened the passenger door, guided me in with his hand to my back, and then shut the door. I watched him make his way around the front and noticed I wasn't putting up too much of a fight. I blamed the threat he offered earlier. At least, that was what I was telling myself.

I bounced my knee up and down as he climbed in the car and started it. He glanced down at my leg, and I stilled it.

Reaching back, I dragged my seat belt around me and clicked it in, and then, a smiling Saint started to drive. My gut played up a storm. I worried I would either fart, shit, or vomit. None would be good.

Glancing to the man next to me, I noticed he tapped some fingers on the steering wheel to the music playing on the radio. He looked calm and collected. I couldn't work the guy out. I'd always thought he was set on his life of the club, businesses, and then the women he picked through to fuck.

Why did he have me in his car and we were driving to his place?

Was it just because I gave good head?

Trying to understand the guy was hurting my brain. But I wasn't sure my heart wouldn't get involved in the process of whatever this was. That concerned me the most.

When we stopped, I took in the area and faced him. "Why are we at the movies?"

He winked. "Thought we'd go see that new action flick."

What. The. Actual. Fuck?

CHAPTER EIGHT
SAINT

*P*oor guy was speechless, and on our first date as well. There wasn't anything I could do. I was used to shocking people, and usually, it was in bed with how good I was. I let him have his time. I got out of the car, went around to his side, and opened the door. He just sat there. It was sweet, really. Leaning in, I undid his seat belt, took his arm, and helped him out of the car.

I shifted him to the side and shut the door, then locked the car.

"We're at the movies," he said.

"Yep, gonna see a kickass action one."

"The movies."

"Damn right." I didn't think it would be a good time to mention it was for our first date. Not since he was taking so long to catch up on the fact. I'd leave it for later. Maybe I'd tell him after he'd had his next reaction when I took him out for a drink after.

With a hand to his lower back, I gently guided him forward to the box office. I bought the tickets, and Kylo was looking around as if it was the first time he'd seen the theater. Then I guided him to the food counter.

"What do you want to eat?"

"Huh?"

I chuckled. "Food and drink, what's your flavor?"

He blinked. "You're seriously takin' me to the movies. This isn't some prank, some game?"

Well, fuck, he'd thought I was messing with him. I shook my head and smiled. "No, Kylo. No tricks here. Now, what do you want?"

He studied me for a moment and then nodded once. He turned to the lady behind the counter. "Pepsi and popcorn, both large. Milk Duds as well."

Then I said, "I'll have the same." I caught Kylo pulling out his wallet, but he stilled when I placed a hand on his arm. He looked up at me. I shook my head and told him, "I've got it."

He nodded and put his wallet back in his pocket. I was just glad he wasn't going to fight me on it. We took our items and moved to hand our tickets to the usher.

Inside, we grabbed a couple of seats in the middle toward the back of the theatre and settled down. "When was the last time you went to the movies?" I asked before eating a handful of popcorn.

Kylo shrugged. "Jesus, I can't even remember. Must have been when I was a teen. I know I never went with my parents. I think Boom and Wendy took me to see something a couple of times."

Christ, I knew he'd come from a shit home, but it twisted my insides thinking he didn't get a normal childhood. I was one lucky fucker to have one.

He opened his mouth and then closed it. "What?" I asked. He shook his head. I knocked my knee against his. "Tell me or ask me."

He gave me side-eyes and then looked back to the screen when the ads started playing. "What about you? For the movies?"

This was good. He was coming back into himself now that the shock had subsided. This was what a normal date was supposed to be like—talking and finding out about each other.

"Couple of months ago. Another action flick I was interested in."

"If you come often, does that mean you know Marvel?"

"Fuck yes. Marvel rocks."

He hummed under his breath.

"What?"

"Nothin'." He was thinking of something that made him smile, and I wanted to know what it was.

"Kylo," I said in a low tone, knocking my knee into his again.

He glanced down, saying, "Was at your place a while ago watchin' Marvel with Lucas because Death and Wreck hadn't seen it before. That's when I found out about Lucas and Wreck datin'."

"Where was I?"

He chuckled. "In bed, oblivious to everythin'."

I nudged him with my arm. "Shut up, man. I'd been busy."

"Hey, if Death hadn't told me, I wouldn't have expected it either. Never would have thought Wreck would go that way."

"Shit, nor me." And I wouldn't have for me either, but I guess it took a special kind of guy to open your eyes to other possibilities. Not that I could say any of that shit. I had a feeling Kylo would get up and leave. He was fighting this for some reason, and I was sure it was because he didn't trust I wanted to see where this could go. He thought I'd go back to women. Fuck, I hadn't even thought of one since the first time. Hadn't been with one since the second time, and that shit said something because I loved fucking. Before Kylo, I'd screwed around nearly every damn day, and since Kylo and I hadn't been around one another for the last few weeks, other than for work, his absence had been getting to me.

Eventually I'd tell him, but when he was used to this—used to me being around him.

"But now I see it's good for them. They're all loved up and lookin' to the future."

"They are," Kylo agreed, and took a sip of his drink before eating more popcorn.

The movie started and I relaxed back a bit more and got into it. But I half focused on Kylo. He laughed when it was funny, he liked it when the action happened, and I could tell he was enjoying himself.

Fuck, it felt good being here with him. Especially as it was something different for him since he hadn't been in so long and was something I loved to do.

By the time the credits rolled through, Kylo had a smile on his face. He turned to me and said, "That was a fuckin' good movie."

I grinned. "Knew it would be." I stood and added, "Maybe next time I'll let you pick though."

"Sure," he said straightaway without thinking. Then his brain caught up. His eyes flashed for a second before he righted them. "Right, we goin'?" He nodded toward the aisle.

"Yep."

He followed me out silently. I didn't know if I should give him time in his head or talk some crap that got him out. I'd let him have it until we got to our next destination.

The drive to the bar was short. I parked down the road and got out.

Kylo's door opened, and he called, "Where we goin'?"

"Gettin' a drink. There's a cool place down the road."

"I'm not really feelin' it."

"Come on, one drink, and then we can go," I said, and started down the path. I heard his door slam closed. I locked the car, and then his footsteps ate up the concrete as he pulled up beside me.

"One drink?"

I winked. "Promise."

"Fine."

I stepped through the door and noted the place was busy, but not packed, which was good. We'd be able to find a place to sit and chat for a while. "Go find a place to park our asses. I'll get us a beer." Kylo nodded, and I watched him make his way over to the far right where there was a spare booth.

I grabbed our drinks and took them over. Once I placed his on the table and got a thank-you, I sat and scooted around to sit closer to him. I noted his pulse in his throat ticked up faster. I smiled to myself and took a sip. When Kylo took a gulp, I noticed how his throat moved and wanted to know what it would be like to shift in and kiss him right there.

Shaking my head, I glanced away and around the bar. I couldn't deny it—I wanted to know what everything felt like with Kylo. I'd never kissed a guy. I wondered if it would be so different to a woman—already getting a blow job was, but what about fucking? What would it feel like to slide into his ass?

My cock throbbed from the thought.

"What're you thinkin'?" Kylo asked.

I snorted. "You don't want to know." I glanced at him and whatever he saw made him nod. I winked and chuckled.

Kylo cleared his throat. "Did you always think you'd end up where you are?"

"What? In a bar with you?"

He coughed. "No. Just… the business and in the MC?"

"Nah. In high school, I thought I wanted to be a truck driver. Then by the end, I knew I wanted to run my own business, but I didn't have a clue how. I went to college for a year on a business degree, but fuckin' hated it. I got out, went from job to job, and then met State and Country one night out where I used to serve drinks. There was a fight. They had each other's backs, but I lent a helpin' hand because I knew they hadn't started it and were outnumbered. This was before the other brothers could get there and help. I was intrigued by the brotherhood. I had friends, but no one I could depend on to have my back like that. I had Lucas, but we weren't so close. Not like we are now. Before State and Country could leave, I approached them, askin' what it took to get into the club. Country patted me on the back and said I'd proved all I had to that night. I became a prospect." I smiled at Kylo. "Did all the shit jobs until I was a full member. It was then I spoke to them about runnin' our own business of pussy. With enough willin' women in the club, they might as well get paid for it." I shrugged. "It took off from there, and not once have I regretted my decisions." I took a sip and looked at him. "When I make my mind up about somethin', I make sure it happens, to get what I want."

Did he understand what I was saying?

By the way he swallowed slowly and how his chest rose and fell quickly, I reckoned he did.

"Things happen for a reason," I said.

He hummed under his breath. "I guess they do, but some things that happen shouldn't, and it needs to stop."

Was he trying to say we needed to stop?

There was no way in hell. I hadn't felt this fucking comfortable on a damn date before. Christ, I hadn't really been on a date. I fucked women, but that was it. We hooked up for sex. I didn't take them places like I wanted to with him.

This wasn't stopping. He'd learn that soon.

"I don't agree" was all I said. "What about you? Did you always want to be a male escort?" I wouldn't call it a hooker because he wasn't one, not since he didn't sleep with his clients. And if I had anything to do with it, which thank fuck I did, he wouldn't be sleeping with a client ever.

Kylo laughed before frowning. I had a feeling he wanted to stay on the conversation of how things shouldn't happen, but too bad. I wouldn't have it as he'd just keep thinking this was all wrong. I would prove to him eventually that women didn't matter to me when all I could think about was him. I had the lust part down. Now I wanted to get to know the man better.

He shook his head. "Hell no, but when opportunities arise to set up your future, I'm goin' to take it. You've heard my sob story and why."

"I'm sure Boom and Wendy would help out if needed."

"That's the thing. I don't want to rely on them. They've done so much for me already by takin' me in. I want to get out on my own two feet. I'm fuckin' twenty-three for fuck's sake. It's time I moved out of home, and to do that, I need money behind me."

I nodded. "I can understand that. But you've been workin' within the compound for ages…."

"You askin' me where the money has gone?" He smirked. "I didn't blow it, well, unless you can call my ride a waste of money."

"Fuck no."

He tipped his drink my way. "There you go."

"You'll be a full member soon. You lookin' forward to it?"

His grin was big. "Yeah, I won't have to take as much shit. But I do like workin' the bar and shootin' the shit." The door opened, and a group of women stepped through. Kylo whistled. "Check them out."

I'd forgotten he was bi, not gay. So then why couldn't he understand I could be bisexual as well? Maybe because it was still new for me and even Kylo. Honestly, I hadn't opened my eyes until him, but I knew for certain at least that I was bi for Ky.

"They're comin' this way," he said, smiling.

Fuck no.

"Hey, guys—"

"Go," I clipped. Kylo's gaze spun to me and he jerked back slightly when he saw I was pissed. He didn't get to smile at them like that, like he wanted their attention and company. Not when I was sitting right fucking there next to him on our first damn date.

Giggles started around us. One said, "Sorry? We just thought you two would like some—"

I moved my hard gaze from Kylo to the women. There were five. They were good-looking, but none of them interested me.

"We ain't after anythin' from any of you."

One huffed. "You don't need to be a dick about it." They turned and walked away. I shot back the rest of my beer and moved out of the booth.

"Let's go."

He didn't move.

I faced him, rested my hand on the table, and leaned in. "Get the fuck up, Kylo. Now." Annoyance and some anger left my chest heavy. We'd been having a good time. We'd been getting to know one another, and then he went and wanted attention from pussy.

Shaking my head, I started for the door. If he followed, I knew he was sorry. If he didn't, then I knew he didn't want something with me.

I went out the door and strode down the path with my hands fisted and jaw clenched. I'd been sure he was into me. He looked at my body a lot like I was something he wanted to lick and keep. Had I made up that he was interested? Was my head that fucking cocky I thought I saw something that wasn't actually there? Hell, maybe he still wanted my brother and I was the replacement.

All that ran through my head but suddenly stopped when I heard heavy footfalls coming my way.

I wasn't stupid. I wasn't making this up. He wanted this, but it was his nerves. He didn't understand me and what I wanted… that messed him up.

He'd come after me, so maybe he was sorry. When he fell into step with me, I knew it even more by the way he went to speak a few times but didn't. Instead, he knocked his shoulder into mine as we reached the car. I glanced at him, and he offered me a small smile and a shrug.

Yeah, he was sorry.

I gave him a chin lift as I unlocked the car and opened his door. He climbed in and I shut his door. Would he think he was going home? That I'd drop him off at Boom and Wendy's?

He'd be wrong.

Not when I had my house to myself. But if he thought we'd be fooling around, he'd be wrong again. I was in the mood to snuggle. I smiled to myself as I walked around the car, because I couldn't wait to see how Kylo took to being the little spoon.

It felt like a date. I was having a hard time thinking it wasn't because he took me to the damn movies and a bar. He knocked back women and got pissed when I checked them out.

Did it mean it was a date? Did it mean he *was* interested in me as more than just a hookup?

Jesus Christ, what was Saint thinking taking me on a date? Maybe my blow job skills had messed up his mind. I knew I had talent in that area but not enough to change a guy. I'd never been with a straight guy before. I'd only hooked up with men from a gay club, so I was totally out of my element with Saint, to a point I didn't know what to believe.

I knew we weren't driving toward my home, but I couldn't point that out verbally. Did it mean he was taking me to his place? Would it be better if I did open my damn mouth and say I wanted to go home? But did I? I had no fucking clue, which was why I stayed silent and let him pull into his drive. He got out. I did the same and followed him up to the front door, where he unlocked it and entered. As soon as I was through the door, he closed and locked it.

He moved off into the kitchen where the only light shined, and I trailed behind him. "Want a drink?" he asked.

"Nah, I'm good," I said, and put my hands in my pockets when he faced me.

His eyes ran over me as his lips twitched. "Come on, then." He walked by me, and I could have gone to the front door, out it, and made my own way home. I didn't. I followed him, heading to where he'd just switched a light on, knowing it was his bedroom.

The room was smaller than mine. It held a walk-in closet down the end of it, a bed beside the closet door, its headboard up against the wall under the front window. Bedside tables sat on each side of the bed, and a dresser sat on the wall next to the closet doors. A TV and an Xbox were on top of the dresser. It was plain but nice. It suited Saint.

I should have been paying attention to Saint, though, and not checking out the room because then I would have seen him remove his boots and tee. He had his thumbs hooked into his jeans when I looked, and he caught my eyes as he slowly slid them down his legs before kicking them off. He climbed into bed with his boxers on and placed his hands behind his head.

"Grab the light before you jump in," he said.

Wait... what the fuck was going on here? Did he think I'd spend the night? Why would he want that? My heart danced in my chest. The hair on the back of my neck rose as my nerves kicked up another notch.

I couldn't stand here like an idiot all night. I either had to walk out or get into bed. If I got into bed, then what? Would we fool around, and then he'd ask me to leave?

I didn't want to question what was happening as then it'd all be out in the open and real. I wasn't ready to hear real. If I was honest with myself, I was a little scared to hear what he wanted, where he wanted this to go. And Jesus, that made me the biggest pussy out there.

"Kylo," Saint called.

"Huh?"

"Stop fuckin' thinkin'. Get undressed, turn off the damn light, and get in bed."

His words pushed me into action. I pulled my tee off, toed off my shoes, took off my socks, and then quickly removed my jeans. I left my boxers on like he had before I switched off the light and slipped under the covers.

The room was dark, but there was enough light coming through the window behind our heads since the curtain wasn't closed. I lay straight and as stiff as a board next to him, blinking up at the ceiling. It wasn't because I didn't want to be there in bed with him. I did. I liked his assertiveness, his confidence. I got off on those things, of someone else taking control. But my nerves were getting the better of me.

Did I make a move? Was that what he was waiting for?

I wasn't sure my nerves would let me reach out and touch him.

Fuck.

I was in Saint's bed. With him.

Never would I have thought I'd be here. Not with Saint.

He rolled my way, and in the next second, he had my body facing toward the door, and he was flush to my back with an arm over my waist.

What was this?

"Saint—"

"Shush, and it's Zion. It's time for sleep."

Maybe I could if there wasn't a hard-on pressing into my ass. My body had a mind of its own and pushed back against it. Also, what was the deal with him wanting me to call him Zion? As far as I knew, the club members only wanted their.... All right, I would not go there. I would not let that thought finish because it was too intense.

He groaned. "No moving. Sleep."

Was he serious? "Are you serious?"

"Yes."

I stilled when I felt his lips on my shoulder and then the back of my neck. There he whispered, "Unless you wanna tell me what you do with that dildo?"

Fuck no.

"I could use some sleep," I said quietly.

His chuckle swept over the side of my face as he leaned up on one elbow. "That's what I thought." He pressed his lips to my jaw. "Now, I like being the big spoon. You good with the little?"

I nodded, but… holy, holy fuck. He actually wanted to go to sleep. With me in his arms. Of course my dick was going to notice—especially when his dick was still hard and up against my ass. How did he expect me to sleep like this?

My mind and body were buzzed.

He lay back down and curled me into him more, sliding his arm under my neck and hooking it gently around my shoulders.

This was hugging.

Saint was hugging me like he'd done it a million times.

He kissed the back of my neck. "Relax."

"How?" I said before I could stop myself.

I felt his smile on my skin. "Sleep'll come. We just gotta relax."

"You're huggin' me like I'm your own personal teddy bear, but you're pressed so tight I can feel *everythin'.*"

He laughed. "It'll go down eventually. Just relax. Tell me what it's like livin' with Boom and Wendy."

He was good; that was an instant boner killer. Except, as I spoke, his hand over my waist started running up and down my side.

"You touchin' me like that won't help the situation. Even when I'm talkin' about Boom."

His laugh was louder. "Got it." He slid it back over me. "Let's get some shut-eye then. But I just wanna say I'm glad you have them in your life. Glad Boom took you in."

"Yeah," I whispered. "So am I."

I didn't think sleep would find me, but it did. I'd have my freak-out another day when it registered that I drifted off in the arms of Zion "Saint" Storey.

As I STRETCHED, sleep evaporated and awareness locked in. I opened my eyes and looked beside me. The bed was empty. I glanced around the room to make sure what I thought happened had, and when I saw Saint's things, I relaxed a little. Only a little, though, because I was still in Saint's house, in his room and bed, after sleeping beside him all night.

Then I remembered when I woke in the middle of the night. I needed to piss something fierce. Saint had still been at my back. I managed to move out without him waking and went to the bathroom. It wasn't until I was back in the bedroom that I realized I should have made a dash for it. But then I looked down at Saint. He'd gone to his back when I wasn't there. The blanket was down at his waist, his body on display for me to look at with the moonlight shining in.

Christ, he was stunning.

I didn't want to run then. I didn't want to fear the next day and what would happen. So I lay back down. Only I did it facing him, and I even scooted closer, slowly and gently resting my hand on his chest. When his hand covered mine, I froze, but his breath was even. He'd still been asleep, and I closed my eyes, listening to him breathe and found my own slumber.

Only now was *now*, and I didn't know if it'd be best to sneak out the front door since it was right next to Saint's bedroom.

I could hear him moving around out there, and my pulse raced on the extreme speed. Scrubbing a hand over my face, I sat up and put my feet to the ground while pulling the blanket off me. Saint had been smart to get up early. His morning chub would have gone down, but mine was tenting my boxers as if ready for action. I stood, stretched again, and then paced the room, waiting and willing my cock to go down. I didn't need a piss, thank fuck, since it was hard to with a chubby. I thought of everything I could to shrink that fucker, but it was like it knew Saint was in the other room and wanted to show off for him.

Fuck it.

I had to get out of here.

I grabbed my clothes and dressed quickly in case Saint thought of coming back to the room. I snuck to the closed door and opened it a little. He was in the kitchen. From where his door was situated, I could see him clearly at the stove, only wearing jeans. His hips swayed to the gentle music playing in the background.

Shit, fuck, shit. He was cooking. Obviously making us breakfast. Could I really be a dick and leave? I closed the door and dropped my forehead to it. I couldn't fucking leave. Not after he'd been... damn sweet and everything the previous day. He took me to the movies for fuck's sake, plus a bar, and back to his place where we didn't get off but did something I'd never done with anyone else. We'd cuddled. We'd slept together.

It'd been nice.

Sighing, I ran a hand through my hair and then over my face before opening the door. Saint hearing it, turned. His smile was fucking bright.

"Mornin'," he called.

"Hey," I replied with a chin lift.

"Get your ass to the table. Breakfast is ready." He faced me again with two plates in hand and then took in how I was fully dressed. He snorted. "Were you gonna make a run for it?"

I scoffed and ended up choking. "What? No. I'm just, you know, ready for the day." I sat, and Saint put a plate full of fucking bacon, eggs, and toast in front of me. He set his plate down and took the chair next to mine. But before he plonked his ass down, his hand gripped the top of my hair, and he gently tugged my head back to have my eyes.

He smiled. "Mornin' again," he said. I didn't get to reply because his lips brushed against mine quickly, and I was too stunned to do or say anything as he sat in the chair, still smiling, but it'd turned smug.

What was that?

"Saint—"

He shook his head. "Kylo, it's Zion in here. Zion whenever we're alone."

I widened my eyes. "Will we be alone a lot?" was what came to mind and what just popped out of my damn mouth.

He chuckled. "If I have anythin' to do with it, yeah."

Right... okay.... Fuck.

"I don't get—"

His hand landed on mine, and I stopped talking to look down at it. "Let's just eat and we'll talk about it after. Instead, tell me what shit you like to do in your spare time."

He wanted to know what I did in my spare time.

He seemed like he wanted to know me. I knew I was blocking shit between us because I didn't want it to register in my heart, but I was pretty sure Saint—Zion—was trying to be closer to me. In a way where we'd only be with each other. At least, I thought he was.

I wanted to hope, but until we had more time together, until this was a sure thing, I wouldn't. Even when my heart felt like tiny gorillas were beating at my heart every time he talked or looked my way.

I pushed more shit back in my mind and focused on the food in front of me while I told him about building up an old Harley I had stored in Boom's shed. He listened to everything, adding in his own questions.

Then I admitted another thing I liked to do that no one really knew. "I read sometimes too."

"What do you read?" he asked, finishing off his last bite.

I shrugged. "A bit of this and that."

He smirked, leaning back in his seat. "I didn't see any books in your room that night."

Did he have to mention that night? My dick throbbed when my

mind jumped right to the scene with naked Saint—Christ, Zion, something I wasn't sure I'd get used to calling him since it seemed even more personal than having his dick in my mouth.

I cleared my throat and took a sip of the coffee Sa—Zion got me.

He leaned forward, his elbows hitting the table. "Wait, you've hidden them. Why, Kylo, do you read porn?"

I just knew my face was heating. Zion laughed. I shook my head. "It's not porn."

"Then what do the ladies call it? Romance?"

"Anyway, what do you do in your spare time?" I tried to change the subject.

He wouldn't have it, though. "No, no. Let's get back to the romance stories you read. What're they about? Men and women? Men and men?"

"You're not gonna drop this, are you?"

"Nope."

I sighed. "They're paranormal stories. All types."

"Paranormal? Do you mean like werewolves and vampires?"

I shrugged. "Yeah. Now can we drop it?"

"You'll have to read one to me one night," he said with a fucking cheeky grin.

"Not happenin'."

"Come on. It'd be fun."

"No."

"Please?" He pouted like a little kid.

"Hell to the no, Zion."

He sat back. "At least you called me Zion. So I'll drop it... for now."

"Good." I would have to remember to use his name if I ever needed him to let something go.

"What's your plans for the day? Know you got a client tonight, but you doin' anythin' today?"

I shook my head. My pulse picked up from the way he looked at me. He stood, taking my plate and his into the kitchen. He came back with my phone. "Snagged this outta your jeans, heard it vibratin' this mornin'. Boom."

"Shit," I clipped and took it from him.

He leaned in and kissed my neck, I stilled. "Check 'em, then come join me in the shower."

Did he just ask me to have a shower with him?

"Kylo," he said, his tone rougher. He didn't say anything more until I looked up at him. "Text him back, tell him you're busy helpin' me again, which is why you crashed in my spare room." I nodded. He smiled and ran a hand through my hair before he tugged. "Then I expect you in the shower." He brushed his lips over mine and walked from the room.

Holy motherfucking shit.

Zion wanted me in the shower with him. Naked. My dick was already begging for me to do it.

CHAPTER TEN
SAINT

He didn't know I'd been awake when he got up in the night. I'd expected him to make a dash for it, but he hadn't. He'd come back, and I knew he'd been looking at me, trying to decide what to do. When he'd lain back down, leaning into me with his hand on my damn chest, I'd been fucking thrilled by his choice. So much so, I had to reach out to him for it.

When I'd woke next, with a smile on my face, we were back in the spooning position with me up behind him and my hand tucked between his thighs. My chest inflated, my dick sat snugly between his ass cheeks and jerked, as if telling me he liked where he was. It was then I knew I wanted to do it again and again. I wanted to take him places, spend time with him, and eventually fuck him.

It was different, knowing he was a guy I was into, but it was more than I'd felt being with a woman. I didn't get excited about seeing a chick I was with. I didn't smile when I thought of them. I'd been with women for one thing, and that was to get my dick wet. Their company was okay, but Kylo's was something more. So yeah, it might be strange me being with a guy, but even in this small amount of time, it meant something more to me than it ever had before.

That said, Kylo was worth it.

And I'd do anything I could to make sure this happened between us.

Christ, I wanted him so damn bad, but I was still going to take it slow—even though I'd asked him to take a shower with me. We could touch, taste, but I wouldn't be inside him until I knew he was over being freaked out and wanted this with me. For real.

But all I could think was Kylo Lee was mine. Hell, the way he'd walked out all dressed but with sleepy eyes, had my blood rushing. I wanted to reach out, take him in my arms, and kiss the fuck out of him. It was hard not to. But soon, if he'd come to the bathroom, I would have the opportunity to do just that.

Turning on the water, I waited for the heat to kick in before adjusting it to the right temp. I removed my jeans and boxers, stepped in, and closed the glass door. I moved under the spray and let it run over my body while scrubbing my hands through my hair.

By the time I'd washed my hair and body, I was sure Kylo wasn't going to join me. I had my head tilted back when I heard the glass door opening. Turning, I rubbed the water from my face and thinned my lips in a smile, so I didn't fucking moan from seeing Kylo standing naked before me.

His body was only a little smaller than mine but damn fit. His skin was darker, his hair messy from removing his tee. His hands shook, his nerves getting the better of him, or it could be the fact I hadn't taken my eyes off him.

I'd *felt* his dick before, but I'd never seen it. He was thick and at a good length when hard, and hell, he was definitely rocking an erection.

"Come here," I ordered gruffly.

He swallowed, nodded, and no doubt talked to himself about something before he slowly stepped forward.

Reaching out, I took hold of his wrist and pulled him the rest of the way into me as I stepped back out of the spray of water so I could warm his back with it. I hissed out a breath, and Kylo made a noise when our dicks rubbed against each other. It hadn't gone down since waking with him in my bed.

I ran one hand to the back of his neck, the other at the side. He looked at me and licked his lips. Yeah, he fucking wanted this. Wanted me. Wanted a taste.

"Kiss me," I demanded.

When he dropped his hands to my waist, he tipped his chin back slightly and brushed his lips against mine, then pulled back.

"Not enough," I stated, and then tugged him back in and took his mouth in a hot and heavy kiss. Our hands gripped and trailed over each other. I'd even taken hold of his ass and tugged him to me, so his hard cock could grind against mine as our tongues tangled and tasted for the first time.

His head dropped back, and he gulped for breath as I kissed down his neck.

"Zion," he whispered, and I rewarded him for using my name by sliding a hand between us and wrapping it around both our erections. He groaned and dropped his head to my shoulder. It didn't stay there long, though, not when I slid my hand up and down our dicks. He pulled his head up and locked his lips to mine, nipping at my bottom lip.

Fuck me.

Just that one nip had my balls drawing up.

He trailed his mouth down so he could bite my neck, which had me shuddering. He sucked and moaned around my skin.

"Fuck yeah, Kylo." I ran my hand faster over both of us. "Feel that. Feel our dicks together, how we're gettin' off. Hell, Kylo, I didn't know it'd be this good." I kissed his neck. "Didn't know just havin' your dick against mine would drive me goddamn crazy. Fuckin' love it. Your body is made of sin, and I'm wantin' it more and more."

His hands tightened on me. One at my waist, the other at my back, holding me close. He liked me talking, liked hearing my words, and I liked fuckin' sharing them.

"Give me your mouth, Kylo. Want to taste you while I'm feelin' you," I ordered. He licked all the way up my neck and our mouths clashed. Our lips pressed and moved, our tongues slid and glided over and around each other's, and I couldn't get enough of it.

His body tensed. He whimpered against me, his dick thickening right before he lost his load. I broke the kiss to look down between us and see the end of it, which brought mine charging forward. I gripped the back of Kylo's neck, tugged him forward to touch my forehead against his as I came over Kylo and the tiled shower floor.

"Fuck," I uttered.

Kylo hummed under his breath. He dropped his head to my shoulder as I released my hold on both of us. I kissed his neck. I fucking loved kissing him. His mouth and mine were made for each other, and I was sure I'd soon have him realizing we'd be good together.

I ran my hands up and down his back, and he cuddled into me more. "Let's get cleaned up," I suggested. He sighed as if he didn't want to move. I grinned. "What about a ride today? Or we could watch some movies?"

He lifted his head and I saw he was blushing. He was damn sweet. I kissed the side of his mouth and then reached out for the soap, running it over his body. He stood there and watched me, his eyes hooded, his breathing ragged. His dick twitched when I cleaned him, even though he'd just come.

Gently, I pushed him back under the water fully and scrubbed him free of suds. Tugging him back out, I took the shampoo and squirted some into my hand.

"Zion," he whispered. I glanced up at him and could tell this right here was too much. He was feeling it, me taking care of him, me wanting to take care of him. Christ, I'd never done this for another person. Somehow Kylo was different for me. I didn't know how or why, but I was enjoying it, and I wouldn't give it up.

I just hoped he'd accept this—*us*—eventually. From the way he allowed me to do everything I had, it was a good indication he would.

As soon as the last of the conditioner ran from his body, I shut off the water. With a last kiss pressed to his shoulder, I moved around him and got out of the shower. I grabbed a towel and handed it to him before I took mine, and we dried ourselves.

"A ride would be good," Kylo said as he wrapped the towel around his waist. His gaze wouldn't quite meet mine. It seemed his emotions or thoughts were overtaking him again. "But I should get back to Boom's and—" He stopped when I backed him up against the sink.

"You like me."

"I—"

I shook my head. "You don't need to say anythin' to it. I know you do, and that's not me bein' cocky, but my eyes have been opened, and I've seen the way you enjoy my touch. If you want to go home and get your head together before work, then you can. But just don't lie to me about you doin' somethin' you don't have planned."

He swallowed, his eyes wide, and then he nodded. "Okay... I... shit, I just need to go home to think."

I smiled. "All right then, you can have your time, but I want you to know that I like what we have goin' on." With that, I closed my eyes and kissed him hard and heavy before stepping back and heading out of the bathroom to my bedroom to get dressed.

I'd take him home so he could think. I didn't want to overwhelm him and I sensed I was with all these changes. He'd get used to it, but until then, I'd have to be patient.

I was having a second cup of coffee when Kylo walked from the bedroom.

"You ready?" I asked.

He opened his mouth, closed it, and stared at me for a moment before saying, "How about a movie, and then I'll head back to Boom's?"

My damn heart swelled inside my chest. I was sure even my chest expanded.

Playing it cool, though, I said, "Sounds good." I smiled behind my coffee mug.

"You got one for me?" he asked, nodding toward my cup.

"Yeah, Kylo." I winked. "Go get the movie app up on the TV. I'll make it and bring it in."

He nodded and turned while I watched him walk over to the couch, pick up the remote from the coffee table, then sit. He didn't select a single chair. He took the couch, where he knew I'd be sitting next to him.

Fuck me.

Happiness had my gut going nuts like there was a circus in there. He'd wanted to stay longer. Wanted my time more. That right there was progress, and hell, it was good to see that he wasn't running and getting lost in his mind.

I made him a coffee and took it into the living area. "Picked one?"

"You can," he said, taking hold of the mug I held out to him.

"I picked last night, your turn," I told him, then laid down on the couch with my head resting on his thigh. To start with, he'd tensed, but when I rolled to see the TV, he relaxed and went back to searching through the movies.

"Can't go wrong with this. It's a classic, but good one, right?"

"Fuck yeah. Bruce Willis kicks ass in *Die Hard*. You'll have to come back to watch the rest of them with me now we're startin' this one."

There was a beat of silence and then came softly "Yeah."

My damn smile was big.

It wasn't until halfway through that I felt a tentative hand slide to my hair, and Kylo brushed his fingers over my scalp, gently scratching. Hell, if I were a cat, I'd be purring.

A little after that, I was completely relaxed and lazily asked, "Favorite color?"

Kylo snorted, his fingers stilling for a second before he kept going. "Are you seriously askin' this shit?"

"Yep," I said, popping the *p* at the end.

"All right, I think."

I nudged his knee with my hand. "Come on, play along. It's get-to-know-you time."

He sighed. "Fine. I don't really have a favorite color."

Groaning, I said, "Everyone has one. Mine's dark blue. Yours?"

"Same."

Rolling my eyes, I dropped that question. "Okay then, what's your favorite flavored ice cream?"

"Chocolate." I nudged him again. He sighed, then asked, "You?"

"Vanilla. What type of music do you like?"

I felt him shrug. "A bit of everything besides opera."

I laughed. "Well, there goes my idea of taking you to a show."

He chuckled. "Can you imagine? Us walkin' into the theater together… everyone would think we're in the wrong place."

"I think it'd be kinda cute. We could both dress up and fall asleep durin' it." I grinned when he chuckled again. "Did you like sleepin' beside me last night?" I threw in.

He stilled, even his fingers, but then they started back up before he whispered, "Yes."

"What year did you go up to in school?" I asked to help him relax once more, and he did.

"I went all the way in high school. Just didn't go to college because I wasn't interested in it. I liked workin' at the gym."

"Was talkin' to Boom the other day, he said you're good at fixin' things. Cars, bikes, and anythin' like that. Why didn't you look at gettin' an apprenticeship?"

He shrugged again. "I tried a few places around here, but none of them were wantin' one. I gave up and got busy anyway."

Interesting. Maybe if he had a place to work on vehicles, it'd be something he'd want since Boom also said Kylo enjoyed doing it. It was something to think about. Could be another business opportunity.

"Tell me somethin' I don't know about you," I asked.

He hummed under his breath, thinking of something. "You tell me somethin' first while I think."

"All right. I like to play the guitar."

"For real?"

"Yeah, I have one in my room in the back of the closet. Mom and Dad had me take lessons when I was young and in school. It stuck, and I liked it, so kept goin'."

"Will you play a song for me?"

"One day."

"And no one knows?"

"Nah, never had an opportunity to play it around anyone since I keep the guitar here."

"You should bring it to the compound. The brothers would get a kick outta it."

"Maybe I will. Now, about you?"

"I like to draw," he admitted.

"Draw what?"

"Things."

"Kylo, come on, what do you draw?"

"Characters. Like comics."

"That's cool."

"Yeah, maybe." He didn't seem to believe it, though.

"Has anyone seen any?"

"No."

"Then why do you sound like you're not sure about your comics if no one has said anything bad about them?" His hand moved from my hair when I twisted to look up at him. "You don't trust in what you draw?"

Kylo rested his hand on the top of my arm. He rolled his eyes. "I like it enough…. I just never shared it with anyone, and I'm not sure how people would take it."

"You'll show me one day?"

He gave me a small, soft smile. "Maybe when you play the guitar for me."

"Deal." I paused for a beat and then asked, "Can we talk about that dildo yet?"

His eyes widened. His cheeks shot to red, and he pushed me off the couch. I laughed and said, "I'll take that as a no." I got to my knees.

"That's a hell no, and we're never talkin' about it again."

"Bullshit. We will one day." I winked. "For now, how about we make out before I take you home?"

The blush deepened. Fuck, he was too damn sweet. "Sure," he said softly. In case he thought to take it back, I was up on the couch and pulling Kylo into my lap with a yelp before I tugged him close and claimed his mouth with mine.

There was a tiny fucking unicorn frolicking in my gut when I walked into work that night. It galloped around and caused my pulse to race from my heart jumping, knowing I was about to see Zion.

The day had blown my damn mind wide open, only to get stuffed full of everything Zion. His hands, his legs, his face, his body... all of him was cemented in my mind. I had to give myself a pat on the back, though, because, even though I'd been about to shit myself after Zion asked me to shower with him, I still managed to get undressed and in the bathroom without fainting from lack of oxygen.

I'd showered with Zion.

We'd been damn naked again in a room with a light on. Christ, he was hot. It was no wonder my dick hadn't gone down that morning with what happened in the shower... seriously hot. He'd handled my body like a professional. Like he'd been with a guy a million times over and knew what to do and say to get us off.

Of course, it had freaked me the fuck out.

My goddamn feelings were coming out to play, and they wanted to keep Zion, for him to belong to them. I'd been ready to bolt, to get the fuck out of there and hide for the rest of my life.

However, I knew if I pussied out, I would regret it, which was how we ended up on the couch together, talking, watching a movie, and then kissing like we were teenagers.

It'd been fucking brilliant.

"Hi, Jack," Monique, the front desk girl, said with a wink. She knew my name wasn't Jack, but we used our fake names in case any of our clients were present.

"Hey, Danni. How you doin', beautiful?"

"Good." She smiled. "Hope you have a great night."

I did too. I sent her a two-finger wave and headed for Zion's office door. I knocked, but before I got a response on the other side, I opened the door and stopped still.

The unicorn disappeared from my gut and was replaced with lead.

A woman was on her knees in front of Zion's desk, and beside her was a man standing with a gun pointed at Zion.

"Kylo, leave," Zion growled.

The gun aimed my way. "Get the fuck in here."

"No!" Zion snarled. "This is between us. He goes."

The guy still had the gun aimed my way, but he glanced back to Zion and then smiled. "I don't think so. I seem to have all the power here. Things go *my* way." With his free hand, he grabbed the hair of the woman and drew her head back harshly. She let out a cry. It was then I saw her face for the first time.

Heaven. A quiet and shy woman who worked here. I hadn't seen much of her, but every time I did see her in passing, she looked away from me, which told me how shy she was.

Fuck. Had she brought this problem in, or did it follow her because of her looks?

I stepped into the room and closed the door. Zion's jaw clenched. He didn't want me in here, but what did he expect? That

I'd run for safety when he was in here on his own? It wasn't happening. I couldn't leave him to deal with this fucker.

No matter what this was about, I would have his back.

Leaning against the door, I asked, "What's goin' on?"

"Get over here. Stand next to Saint."

He still had a grip on Heaven's hair, so I listened and walked over to lean back against the wall to the side of Zion's office chair, where he sat.

"What do you want, Steve?" Zion demanded in a cold tone.

"More money," he stated and gave Heaven another shake, causing her to whimper.

"What do you mean?" Zion asked.

"I know she makes more than she's bringin' home. She said you guys keep it. I want what's owed."

Anger filled me. I straightened, my hands at my sides fisted. His gaze swung to me when I said harshly, "You mean to say you're her dad, and she's workin' here because you want her money?"

"Kylo," Zion warned.

I ignored it and snarled, "Well?"

Zion turned enough to look up at me, but I didn't take my eyes away from goddamn Steve.

He laughed. "What's it to you?"

"You see, I got a problem with parents making their kids do shit they don't want to do."

He waved the gun around. "Seems like I got the upper hand here. I don't need to say shit."

"He's my boyfriend," Heaven whispered. Steve dropped his hold on her hair to backhand her. She cried out and dropped to the floor. I took a step their way until Zion's hand shot out, stopping me. I ground my teeth together as fury slammed into me. Why the fuck was Zion allowing this shit to go on? This place was locked down like Fort Knox. How did this motherfucker get through in the first place?

And seriously, Heaven could do so much better than this fucker.

"Touch her again, and you'll pay in more blood than you already owe us," Zion snarled.

Steve threw his head back and laughed. "That right? I don't see anyone running to the rescue. I fucking own this situation. I know you got a safe in here. Open it, give me the money owed, and I'll be on my damn way." He waved the gun between Zion and me.

"Just fuckin' relax," Zion barked.

Steve kept his gun on Zion and I didn't like it at all. My feet twitched to move in front of him and my hands clenched to stop from grabbing Zion and pulling him behind me.

Christ, if anything happened…. I couldn't even think of it.

"Move," Steve yelled.

"You keep yellin', you'll alert people."

Steve tapped his forehead with the tip of the gun and then moved it back to Zion when he said, "See, I don't think you're takin' me serious."

The gun fired. I dove for Zion and took him to the ground, while cursing over and over, "Fuck, fuck, fuck."

Then chaos erupted.

Doors opened. Heaven screamed. Steve yelled. Another shot fired before Death took him to the ground, and a heap of other brothers surrounded them to help.

"Zion, fuck. Zion?" I leaned back and saw crimson on his arm. "He shot you," I whispered as I moved my gaze from his arm to his eyes.

Eyes that held humor.

What the fuck?

I ground my teeth together and snarled. "The cunt fuckin' shot you. Made you bleed." In the next second, I was on my feet. As I strode over, while Death stood with Steve, I spotted his gun on the ground. I picked it up, aimed, and the shot rang out around the room. Curses erupted, Steve cried out and hopped on one foot since the other one had a fucking hole in it.

I moved and got in his face. "You fuckin' think you can come in here and shoot him? Think again, you motherfuckin' cunt." I jabbed my fist into his stomach. He bent forward as much as Death would allow him.

Turning, I handed the gun off to Tech and went back over to Zion, where he was leaning against the wall, his good arm cradling the other. I didn't register how quiet the room had gone, until Death started barking orders.

The last part I heard, "—get Lucas here to stitch up his brother. We'll take care of this fucker ourselves."

I kneeled before Zion and glared at his smile. "You like me," he muttered.

"Fuck off."

He chuckled, wincing when it pulled at his arm. "You do. Like a lot."

"Shut it," I ordered, then glanced away from his dancing eyes. How could he be so calm about being shot? My gaze landed on Tech, helping Heaven to her feet as she sobbed. He led her out the room, and I saw Death had handed Steve off to someone else as the prick wasn't in sight and Death was. The brother was looking down at Zion and me while he spoke with Quake.

"We had it under control," Zion said, and I swung my narrowed gaze his way.

"Under control?" I clipped. "How the fuck was it under control? You got shot, that fucker manhandled Heaven, and he walked in here in the damn first place with a fuckin' gun."

He smirked. If he wasn't injured, I would punch the dick. "As soon as the fucker entered, we were on him. I told Death I wanted to play it out. Death was in the bathroom over there with Quake and Tech, but you might not have seen them storm in since you were all over me."

I opened my mouth, snapped it closed, and growled under my breath. Zion snorted, then winced. He reached out and ran a hand over my thigh. "Relax. I'm okay. Things worked out."

I clenched my jaw and then bit out, "If they worked out, you wouldn't be bleedin'."

He waved it off. "It's a flesh wound."

My head suddenly felt like it was going to explode.

I wanted to throttle him, kiss him, punch him, hug him, and scream at him because there was a fuckload of blood for a flesh wound.

Instead, I got up and walked away before I did anything I would regret. I heard his chuckle before he called my name, but I ignored it and kept going. I would wait outside until Lucas showed. Maybe I'd be cooled enough to see Zion again.

Why the fuck he risked his life to let this shit play out I didn't know, but I'd find out because I would stop him from doing it again. He didn't risk his life over anyone's. *Not fucking now and not ever.*

Heaven was a great woman, sweet as pie, but she wasn't Zion, and he was mine, dammit.

Fuck.

Groaning, I scrubbed a hand over my face and leaned against the wall outside Zion's office.

It dawned on me then that I thought of Zion as mine.

He'd wormed his way in, showed me how it could be with him—with a man who hadn't been with a man before. Yet he'd touched my fucking heart in the way where I'd claimed him subconsciously.

Now I knew, could I accept it?

Christ, I didn't have a damn clue. All right, that wasn't true. I wanted him. I wanted him as mine, but I was fucking chilled to the bone at the thought of this just being something Zion was testing out. I needed him to be sure, and one day maybe he'd voice he wasn't playing, testing, but, if I had to guess, it wouldn't be for a while.

Still, I wanted to enjoy what we had, except that was another worry because if I did, I'd be more invested in him. I'd want to keep him for-fucking-ever.

"How long you and Saint been messin' around?" Death asked as he lit a smoke and leaned against the wall beside me. I jolted, lost in my own thoughts, so I hadn't heard his approach.

"What you talkin' about?" I tried but knew I was screwed when I caught Death smirking.

He flicked his lighter on and off. "Really?" he drew out.

"Go annoy someone else," I grumbled.

He let out a bark of laughter. "You think, a prospect as you are, can talk to me that way?"

Shit.

"No disrespect, Death."

"Know that, but you still ain't givin' me an answer."

"Again, no disrespect, but steer your question to Saint."

"Hmm, maybe I will." He pocketed his lighter and clasped my shoulder. "Good job in there, prospect."

"Prospect?" Country called as he made his way toward us. "Fuck, I heard what happened, and the next club meetin', we're patchin' you in, Gun."

"Gun?" I asked.

"Your club name. Tech was goin' on about how you took the gun and handled it like you were born to. So, Gun it is."

My chest expanded. I nodded, then shook the hand of our president when he held it out. "Great work," Country said before walking into the room. "Well, fuck, Saint, that's a lotta blood to get out." I heard.

"Welcome to the club, brother," Death said as Lucas raced into the building.

"Where is he?" he demanded.

"In there," Death said and thumbed to the room. Lucas ran inside. I waited a beat and saw Wreck enter, knowing he wouldn't be far from his man. He also carried a bag of what I expected were supplies.

Death snorted. "He forgot his shit before runnin' in here?"

Wreck grunted, gave us a chin lift, and followed Lucas into the room. I wasn't far behind with Death at my back, and we listened to the end of Lucas's rant, "—you're an idiot, Zion, and wait until Mom finds out. She's going to shoot you herself."

"Lucas, bro, you can't tell her."

Lucas just hummed under his breath and opened the bag Wreck placed on Zion's desk since Zion sat in his office chair.

"Lucas," Zion warned. "You say one word to Mom, and I'll—"

"What?" Wreck asked.

"Fuck," Zion cursed. "Nothin' because Wreck would kill me."

Lucas beamed. "That's right… but, for now, unless you make me upset again, I won't say anything."

Huh, since it seemed Zion was afraid of his mother, I might use that later when I yelled at him for putting his life on the fucking line. Lucas didn't let up his ranting while he stitched Zion up. Whenever Zion complained, Lucas would say, "Suck it up."

Death, Country, and Quake chuckled. I didn't because I was still pissed at him. As Lucas was finishing up, the cleaners came in and got to work. They were paid well to keep their mouths shut. I'd heard that at one of the club meetings.

"As your doctor for the night, I'm ordering you home to rest." Lucas glanced back at Country. He was smart to get the go-ahead from him.

"State's already upstairs for his shift to start early. Listen to your doctor, Saint, and that's an order."

"Fuckin' fine." He glanced over to me. "Prospect, you're givin' me a lift."

It was lucky I took Boom's car instead of my ride.

"He won't be a prospect for long," Country announced. "We're patchin' him in as Gun."

Zion grinned over at me. "Cool name, brother."

I gave him a chin lift. "Won't be able to take you home, brother. Got a client tonight," I reminded him. His grin dropped a little, but he pushed it back on.

"Right." He nodded.

"Wreck and I will drop you home," Lucas put in.

"Yeah, thanks, bro, that'd be good."

Country turned to me. "Why don't you head up to State? He'll get you organized."

"Sounds good." I gave a wave to the room and left. I didn't linger on Zion, even though I wanted to.

It wasn't until I reached the floor State, Wreck, and Country had their office on did I get a text.

Zion: You're coming here after.

My grip on my phone tightened. If he thought he could order me the fuck around after scaring the shit out of me, he had better guess again.

Zion: Please. I need snuggles and I'm cold without my boo by my side.

My lips twitched, but I fought the smile over his idiocy. Hell, I wanted to, but… ah, fuck it.

Me: I will if you never say shit like that again.

Zion: Even though I know you liked it, I won't. Later, lover.

Jesus, what the fuck had I got myself into with him?

CHAPTER TWELVE
SAINT

I must have dozed off, because the next time I woke, there was a hot guy standing over me, holding up the key I'd left out for him.

"Anyone could have fuckin' grabbed this and come in here to kick your ass."

Of course, it just made me grin and realize Kylo needed snuggles more than I did. He probably hadn't admitted to himself that he adored me so much that the whole situation at work had freaked him out, and I wasn't going to bring it up with him yet.

"Come here," I ordered, flinging back the covers with my good arm. It was then I took him in. He was in his casual clothes after his client. His hair was still damp from the shower he would have taken at work.

"Did you hear what I said?" he demanded.

"I did, and I think it's the best time to hug it out." I patted the bed again. He growled under his breath and ran a hand over his head and back again to scrub down his face. "Come on, hop in, and we can talk about it."

"No." He shook his head. "I'm goin' home."

I raised a brow. "Are you really gonna make me get out of bed to chase after you?"

He sighed, nibbled on his bottom lip, then cursed, "Fuck." He paused another beat before starting to remove his clothes. Unfortunately, he kept his boxers on. He turned out the light and slid under the covers. Once beside me, he said, "I'm only doin' this so you don't come after me and fuckin' hurt yourself again."

"Uh-huh, now come closer." I smiled.

He grumbled something under his breath but moved over enough I could curl my arm around his shoulders and hug him to me. He rested his head on my shoulder. I hummed, enjoying him being close. Feeling his cool naked skin against mine. It didn't bother me there were no breasts pushing up against me or that his leg was hairy as he slowly, almost apprehensively, moved it over mine.

I liked Kylo as he was. Even when he had a dick and no pussy.

Go figure.

I grinned into the night, though enough light shined through from the opened curtains. I'd never contemplated being with a guy before. Never really noticed one in a sexual way. It wasn't until Kylo started talking about how good he was at head that my dick had jerked at the words.

I knew a good-looking guy when I saw one, and Kylo was one. That was a bonus for my attraction toward him, but it was after finding out more about him, the shit he'd been through and the man he was now, that had me wanting to be around him. I wanted to know everything there was about Kylo, and it'd only been a month since this shit started between us.

Christ, I was addicted.

It was crazy, yet damn exciting at the same time.

"Zion," he clipped.

"Hmm?"

He sighed again, his breath blowing across my chest. "You said we'd talk about it, so I'll start. Why the fuck did you risk your life for that to play out? Why did you leave a key out front where anyone could have seen you place it there and got in to fuckin' harm you?"

My body warmed, knowing his questions were all about him being worried for me.

Kylo liked me, and I enjoyed knowing that fact.

I traced my fingers over his shoulder. At first, he tensed before finally relaxing. "It'd been set up with Heaven. She needed to get rid of her old man but didn't know how to do it. When Death came up with the idea, he told her to get him into work. We had it handled. Knew somethin' could happen, but it'd be small compared to what she'd been dealin' with at her place. He wouldn't leave her, Kylo. Abused her verbally and physically. No woman needs that in their life. Not when we could stop it. So it's done."

"Done with you gettin' shot."

I gripped the top of his hair and tugged his head back to have his eyes. Eyes that darkened from the firm hold and had me wondering if my Kylo liked rough play. My gut clenched in excitement from the thought. "Like you carin', Kylo. A damn lot. But we're in the same club. We work at the same place and both know there's gonna be risks in those."

He ground his teeth together. "Yeah, but why you?"

"Would it have been fair if it was Death? Or Wreck? Or Country? It just happened to be me there on the night he dropped in. I was prepared to get to the bottom of it, to stop other shit happenin'. Even though we're doin' what we do, bein' involved won't stop me from makin' decisions like that, not if I can help someone who can't help themselves."

"I fuckin' hate that I understand your reasonin'."

Chuckling, I pressed my lips to his, and the way his eyes widened a fraction told me the quick kiss surprised him, even when he was in my bed mostly naked.

"About the key, I won't leave it out if you take it with you. It's a spare one."

His body tensed. "Zion," he muttered.

I clamped his lips together between my thumb and finger. His eyes narrowed as I smiled. "Nope. Don't want to hear it. Just take it. You don't have to use it, but it'd save me gettin' bitched out if I leave the key out for you again."

It was impressive how his eyes narrowed even more. He mumbled under my fingers. I let go and asked, "Yes?"

"Fine," he clipped.

"Good. Now, my doctor said I had to get some rest. You gonna let me, or we could talk some more. You could tell me about that dildo?"

He snorted. "Shut up and go to sleep, Zion."

Laughter dropped from my mouth. "You'll tell me one day exactly what you do with it. For now, I'll sleep if you kiss me first."

"You annoy me," he growled.

"Nah, you like me."

"Whatever," he said before he leaned in and took my mouth in a searing, dick-jerking kiss. One I wanted all the damn time. We both pulled away panting, and somehow during the kiss, I'd pulled him more on top of me.

He cursed and complained about how he was going to hurt me, but hell, I'd take all the pain in the world if he kissed me exactly like that.

WINCING, I woke in pain. I must have shifted and pulled at my arm. Still, even when I wasn't moving, it burned like a bitch.

"You okay?" a groggy voice asked.

I blinked and noticed it was early hours. I glanced beside me and found Kylo just about in the same position he'd been in when we'd fallen asleep, lying close to me with his leg and arm over me. Only his head was on the pillow and not my shoulder. I swallowed. "Yeah, woke to it throbbin'."

He snorted.

I grinned. "Not talkin' about my dick, lover."

His kiss to my shoulder had my heart squirming. He got to an elbow. "Did Lucas give you anythin', or you got some pain pills around somewhere?"

"There's some in the bathroom." I made a move to sit up until Kylo pushed me back with a hand to my chest.

"Stay, I'll get it." He slipped out of bed, his feet slapping down on the hardwood floor as he walked down the hall.

It'd been only *two* nights I'd had him in my bed, and already I knew I wanted more with him. I liked knowing he was here, enjoyed seeing him when I woke. Was this moving too fast? I didn't know, but I wasn't stressing over it. I was a "go with the flow" type of guy.

Did Kylo know that he was the only person I'd had sleep over? I wondered what he'd think if he did know. Would he freak and walk out, thinking it was too serious, too fast? He could, which was why I wasn't going to say anything.

I doubted I could even explain it right anyway if he asked why it was him and not any of the others, because I wasn't sure myself. But I didn't feel the pressure from being with him I felt with women.

Kylo entered and waved a packet of painkillers my way. "You right to sit?"

I nodded and showed him how good my abs were by pushing the blankets down, so he was free to see them work when I slowly sat up in a crunch.

He rolled his eyes. "Very impressive."

I winked. "I thought so."

He picked up the glass on my bedside table I'd filled the night before as I shifted back to lean against the headboard. I took the drink of water, then the tablets he held out. I swallowed them and put the glass back down.

"Get back into bed. It's too early."

"Or I could head home and help Boom clean out the garage. He's been bitchin' about it forever."

I was already shaking my head. "Nope. You need to pay attention to me all day since I'm hurt."

He blinked slowly. "I need to pay you attention because you're hurt."

Cocking my head to the side, I asked, "Didn't I just say that?"

"Why?"

"Why what?"

"Why do *I* need to pay *you* attention?"

I chuckled. "Because you like me."

He groaned and dropped his head back to stare at the ceiling.

"And because you're my boo-boo bear, who wants to dote on me." I went to raise my arm and dramatically winced. It hurt a little, but not enough it'd stop me from doing things. Still— "Oh, that hurt. How will I shower on my own? How will I feed myself?"

I opened my eyes; he was already glaring down at me. "Seriously?"

Smiling, I nodded.

His lips twitched. "You're a fuckin' fool."

However, he didn't leave. "I'm your fool though."

His jaw ticked, and I knew I'd gone too far. He didn't see me as his yet. He needed more time to know I wasn't going to run to the next woman who showed me some tits.

"I'm gonna get some coffee," he said. I gave him a soft smile and nodded. Again, at least he wasn't leaving. I watched him walk from the room and rested my head back against the headboard, sighing.

I'd prove to him I wanted to give us a go. One day he'd realize I was serious, maybe in a week, a month, even a year, but I'd wait and enjoy the ride we were on along the way.

I swung my gaze toward the door when I heard footsteps on the front porch. I flicked the covers back and got out of bed when I heard a key being inserted in the lock. I rounded the bed and kicked Kylo's clothes under the bed when I listened to the front door being swung wide. Then I thought about why the fuck I hid his clothes when he was standing in the kitchen anyway. Not that I would have hidden them for my sake. I was thinking of Kylo, knowing he wouldn't want a brother to see him half naked in my house.

"Zion, my boy" was called loudly as my mom and dad walked into the house.

Mom spotted me first, her eyes widening, and she cried out, "Zion, your arm," before rushing me.

"Mom, I'm fine."

"What happened?" Dad asked while Mom shook me a little. "Jesus, Lucy, he looks injured enough."

"What did you do?" Mom demanded.

"Just a little accident, nothin' to worry about," I told her with a calming smile.

She nodded. "Good." Then she smacked me in the arm—thankfully, it was the good one.

"What was that for?"

"Bull-pooping me. I'm going to make coffee before I throttle you. Then you'll come out and explain." She stormed from the room just as I remembered Kylo. I quickly took off after her.

"Son, she's in a tiff now. You'd better settle her with whatever stupid story you're about to say."

"Yep, will do," I said absently and saw Mom cleaning down the counter. Kylo wasn't in sight, except for the two mugs on the counter. Where he'd disappeared to so quickly, I didn't know.

"Gerry, grab me some more coffee," Mom said when he entered the kitchen. "Zion, sit, and tell me everything."

I didn't really have a choice. She was my mom.

Actually, I did. I could kick them both out if I wanted to live a miserable life and have Mom twist it into a sob story; she would bring it up all the time to torture me.

"Huh," Dad said.

"What?" I asked.

He faced me from the pantry. "Didn't know you could buy that at the store."

My brows dipped in confusion. "What?"

"A half-naked guy." He grinned and stepped back to open the door wider, which was when I saw Kylo. Of course he was blushing red.

"Hey," Kylo said.

Mom spun around and her eyes widened. "Zion, why do you have a man in your pantry?"

I didn't know what I could say without freaking Kylo out. Though I bit my tongue, so I didn't bust a gut laughing my ass off.

Kylo stepped out of the pantry and scrubbed a hand over his face before sucking in a breath and saying, "I'm Kylo, a friend of Lucas and Saint's, also a club member." He held out a hand to Dad, who took it and shook.

"I'm Gerry, Zion's Dad, and the gaping woman over there is Lucy, Zion's mom."

Kylo nodded.

"Are..." Mom started, but then she turned to me. "Is he yours?"

Fuck did I want to yell 'hell yes.' I didn't because Kylo dropped a laugh, which sounded shaky, and he shook his head. "No, we're not... like that, and.... Crap, I just stayed the night to keep an eye on him after what happened." A twinge of hurt brushed through me, but I knew Kylo didn't mean it. He was scared because of my parents.

"What did happen?" Dad asked. Then he leaned into Kylo and whispered—or what he thought was a whisper—"Don't worry if you're gay. We have a son who is, and we're proud of him." He looked at me. "But I never thought you were." Obviously, Dad read Kylo's hesitancy.

I shrugged.

"Wait, are you?" Mom asked.

I opened my mouth to answer, but Kylo clapped. "Right, I think I better get goin'. It was great to meet you both." He nodded and started backing from the kitchen.

"See what you did, Lucy. Scared him away."

"Oh, please, don't leave. I don't mind if Zion's gay. I just wanted to know for certain."

Poor, poor Kylo. His eyes widened in fear. He really didn't know what to do or say. He also didn't know how crazy my family was. Though, he was certainly seeing it now.

Standing, I moved into Kylo, who let out a panicked noise. The noise made me want to laugh again. Previously, he'd been damn fearless in the front of fuckface Steve, yet it seemed parents scared him senseless.

I curled an arm around his waist and ignored his wide eyes when they landed on me. Instead, I said, "Yeah, Kylo and I are seeing where this goes between us, but you can't say anything to anyone."

Another noise fell from Kylo's lips. He tried to bolt, but I held him tight.

Dad smiled. "Our lips are sealed."

Dad and I looked to Mom. "Lucy," Dad warned.

When she said nothing, I said, "Mom."

She rolled her eyes. "Fine, I won't say anything. I'll just have to tell Heather that Zion can't see her daughter since he's taken."

"He's not taken," Kylo blurted, and then slammed his lips together.

Dad chuckled. Mom smiled softly, and I told them, "Don't worry, he *likes* me a lot. We're workin' on everythin' else."

CHAPTER THIRTEEN
KYLO

Zion had lost his ever-loving mind. It had to be the gunshot. Maybe poison had got into his blood and was fucking with his head. He didn't seriously just announce we were seeing each other to his parents… right?

Wait, were we really seeing each other?

Fuck it, we were.

But the situation was an awkward one and had me boiling from embarrassment. I would have preferred to have met Zion's parents when I wasn't half naked.

A knock sounded on the door. In the next blink of an eye, I was grabbed and shoved back in the pantry. I was sure the person who grabbed me was Zion's father.

"Hello," I heard Lucas call.

"Mom, Dad, not a word," Zion whispered.

"Hello, my boy," Lucy yelled.

I heard Lucas walk into the kitchen. Then there was a brief pause before Lucas said, "Where's Kylo? His vehicle's out the front."

Shit, fuck.

"He's asleep in your old room," Zion said quickly.

"Why?" Lucas drew out.

There was another beat of silence. "Because he...."

Crap, maybe I could just walk out of the pantry, which I couldn't believe I was in again, and then Lucas would see me half naked.

Fuck me and my life. This was ridiculous.

"He wanted to check if I was okay since he was involved in the whole episode. He looked tired, so I told him to crash here," Zion explained.

Would he buy it?

"Cool," Lucas said. "I'll just go and see—"

"Wait," Gerry yelled. "Ah, didn't you say, Zion, that he needed all the sleep he could get?"

"That's right," Lucy added. "When we arrived, you said to keep quiet, so we didn't wake him."

Someone sighed, no doubt Lucas because his family sounded a little tense. "Fine. I'm here to check your arm anyway before I go to work."

"You never did tell us what happened to your arm, Zion," Lucy said.

"Yes, Zion, what did happen?" Lucas said, sounding awfully gleeful about it.

"There was a situation at work. Nothin' I couldn't handle."

"What type of situation?" Gerry asked, his voice deep with suspicion.

"Gun," Lucas coughed out.

"What?" Lucy cried.

Meanwhile, I was getting a cramp in my thigh since there wasn't enough room in here, and I was afraid if I moved, I would knock something over.

"Mom, it's fine. Kylo got me out of the way, and then the brothers burst into the room. It was a tiny situation, and one that won't happen again."

Lucy whimpered.

"Jesus, Zion, look what you've done. Lucy, darling, our boy is fine. You can see that."

I heard her sniffle.

"Fucking hell, now she's crying. You're going to pay for this," Gerry yelled. There was a slap, and next Zion cursed. "Comfort your mother, now."

I listened to his soft, reassuring words to his mom. He was lucky to have people who cared so much about him. I knew I had Boom and Wendy, but I didn't have anyone for many years of my life, and unfortunately, those years were embedded in my mind.

"Mom, really, Zion is fine. The situation was taken care of quickly, and now I must check his bandage before I go to work."

"Okay," Lucy whispered, but her voice rose when she added, "But if you ever put yourself in a position like that again, Zion, I'm going to beat you black and blue myself."

"Got it, Ma." Humor filled his voice.

"I love you, Zion."

"And I take that love and double it back to you."

The room fell silent. After a few beats, the pantry door opened, and a grinning Gerry stood there. "They're in Zion's room. If you rush, you can make it to the spare room. Must be uncomfortable in there."

I nodded. "It is." After my thanks, I quietly made my way out of there and down the hall to Lucas's old room. There was a bed made and ready for someone, and a desk, but that was it for the room. I quickly slipped under the covers and rested back with my hands behind my head. Since it was early and I'd only got a few hours of sleep, it didn't take long before my eyes drifted closed.

Yet, I was smiling as I fell asleep.

I was smiling because of the fool in his bedroom with his brother.

He was crazy and had managed to worm his way in, to a point I found his actions sweet. It was unbelievable he'd never been with a guy because he did it with me so well.

It blew my mind he'd said we were together in front of his

parents, which told me how damn serious he was. He would have brushed my appearance away otherwise, especially to them.

My stomach couldn't help but flip in the best kind of way. Hell, it was doing it all the damn time whenever I thought of Zion.

He was real. No, he was *being* real about seeing where this went. I still couldn't fathom his switch, but I wanted to see where this went. Even if he found out, in the end, this wasn't for him, being with a guy, and left me with a broken heart. I wanted it all because Zion made me happy.

"Sleepin' Beauty" was whispered close by, and then I felt fingers brush against my brow. I knew who it was, and my heart gave a thump at the intimate touch. "Kylo," he tried again when I didn't make a sound.

"Hmm?"

"Time to get up, or you won't sleep tonight." He shoved at me, all tenderness gone. Even that had me smiling, but I thinned my lips to hide it. He tapped my forehead. "Come on. We're going shoppin'."

"No thanks," I said, rolling away from him.

"But you have to. How will I push the cart or pick up heavy things?"

It was a mistake when I didn't move because, in the next second, I had a wet finger sliding into my ear. "Jesus, Zion, that's fuckin' gross." I threw the sheet back and stood to get away from him.

"Look, you're up. Go get dressed and we'll head off. I know you don't have anythin' on this afternoon or have a client tonight. We'll grab some beers while we're out and play strip poker later. I'll even let you win a couple of times, so you get to see my awesome body."

Was his head screwed on right?

There wasn't a chance of going back to sleep, and not that I wanted to admit it, but Zion was right. He was correct that if I kept sleeping, I wouldn't that night. Sighing, I said, "Fine. But we're gettin' burgers while we're out."

"Deal." He grinned. "Chop, chop," he added, and when I walked by him, he slapped me on the ass. Rolling my eyes, I shot him the finger over my shoulder and was rewarded with a laugh.

It was good my clothes were clean from the previous night. I stole a pair of Zion's boxers though. He'd find that out later if we did play strip poker.

At the supermarket, I asked, "Tell me why you need to go shoppin' when I spent some time in your pantry, and it looked damn full."

Zion chuckled from behind me as I pushed the cart down the aisle. His hand touched my waist. I stopped, and his breath brushed over my ear when he said, "Maybe I just wanted you to come so I could stare at your ass."

Fuck.

My gut tingled, along with my balls. Even my dick gave a happy jerk behind my jeans.

I grunted and started forward again. Zion laughed. "Why, Kylo, from your blushin' cheeks, I'm thinkin' you liked hearin' that."

"Whatever," I mumbled. I wasn't letting him know how much I liked that he wanted to check out my ass, and I also wasn't thinking about it anymore because if I kept going, it'd lead me into thoughts of Zion and my ass. My dick pulsed again, even at the small thought.

He moved to my side and swung his good arm around my shoulders before giving my cheek a quick peck. "You're fuckin' adorable."

"Great," I said dryly. "Every guy likes to hear that from their—" I thinned my lips, I was about to say partner or boyfriend, but knowing me, it would have come out as parfriend or some shit.

Zion rubbed his nose against my cheek. "Their what, lover?"

"Friend," I said.

He snorted. "Bullshit." His arm dropped from my shoulders to slap my ass. I let out a shocked cry and glared at him.

"Quit it," I clipped.

"Only if you tell me what you were gonna say."

I sighed and looked to the ceiling before shifting my gaze to the side and scowling at the man. "Tell me why I'm hangin' with you again? You're fuckin' annoyin'."

He grinned. "Annoyin' in the best way, and besides, we already worked out you like me, and that right there is the main reason you put up with me."

"Fuckin' hell." I started pushing the cart again. "Are you even lookin' for the food you want?" I asked. Another slap landed on my ass. "Zion," I growled.

"Tell me, or I'll make up my own assumption." He tapped his chin. "Hmm, let me see. You were going to say that every guy likes to hear that from their scrumptious man, from their fella who has the biggest—"

I quickly put my hand over his mouth when a mother and a toddler walked around into our aisle. "Boyfriend. I was going to say boyfriend or partner. Now stop."

Behind my hand, I could feel his mouth tilt up into a big smile. He took my hand from his mouth, kissed my palm, then moved ahead of me, looking at the items on the shelf.

Had the pain meds made him crazier than normal?

Then again, he was always the one to mess around with the brothers.

And even when I felt slightly annoyed, a smile lifted my lips because I fucking loved being around him. Shit, I wasn't sure if I'd been shot the previous night that I'd be in a good mood like him. It was as if nothing could get him down.

After we grabbed a few more things, we stood in line at the cash register, and I kept fighting with myself.

Fuck it. I'd just do it.

I curled an arm around Zion's neck and gently tugged him into my side. His hand landed on my waist, and his eyes met mine.

"I do like you," I told him.

His lips twitched. "I knew it when you shot someone for me." His hand tightened on me. "Like you too, Kylo."

"Next in line, please" was called.

Zion faced the cashier and grinned. "Sorry, can't help it when he distracts me. He's smokin' hot, right?"

The cashier blushed and looked down at the register, then nodded.

Zion chuckled. "Don't worry, darlin'. I know what you're seein', and he drives me crazy."

"Zion, shut it," I bit out as I placed our items on the conveyor belt. My face was burning. Zion made a move to zip his lips. He winked at the cashier, but thankfully, he stayed quiet. Didn't stop him from touching me at the waist, the arm, the shoulder, fuckin' anywhere every time we moved around each other.

Once outside, we started toward my car when I heard yelled, "Kylo?"

Turning, I noticed a woman and a man who stood just outside the supermarket. The woman waved, but the man just stared as he leaned against the wall.

"Oh God, it is you, Kylo," the woman called as she made her way over to us. The man followed more slowly.

As they drew closer, I got a better look at them and froze.

"Kylo?" Zion whispered.

"Look, Henry, it's our boy," Samantha, my fucking mother, said with a smile.

She was fucking smiling like they hadn't treated me like shit for all my time with them.

I felt Zion move closer. His heat reached out to me because I suddenly felt chilled to the damn bone. Never had they sought me out. Never had they contacted Boom or Wendy to find out how their only fucking child was. Yet, here she was, stopping in front of me with a beaming smile, while Henry, my fucked-up father, just stared.

"How are you?" Samantha asked as she scratched at her arm. I took her in then. She looked wrung out, so did Henry for that matter. Both had scabs on their faces and arms. They were still using, but were they selling as well? From their dirty appearance and twitchy actions, I doubted it because when they had been selling, they'd kept themselves well enough for clients to see them.

"What do you want?" I bit out.

"No way to talk to your momma, boy," Henry thought to say.

I leveled him with a glare. "Don't call me boy."

Henry's upper lip rose. "You think you're too good to even talk to us? What, Boom took you in and showered you with love, the type you get after suckin' his dick a few times, and now you're too good for us?"

In a flash, I grabbed his ratty tee and pulled him close. "Never fuckin' speak of Boom in that way again." I shoved him back, and he went a few steps, peddling his arms in a windmill motion. "In fact, I don't want to hear anythin' that comes outta either of your mouths." I turned back around and found Zion scowling at the cockheads.

"Kylo, please," Samantha begged. "Please, just wait. Your dad doesn't mean anythin' he says. He—"

Over my shoulder, I stated, "He ain't my fuckin' father, and you're not my mother. If I see you again, it'll be too soon, and neither of you will like it."

"Do not fuckin' try it, asshole," Zion warned. "Keep goin' to the car, Kylo."

"What, you lettin' him suck your dick too?" I heard Henry say, and Zion clipped something back, but I kept moving on. I didn't realize my hands were shaking in rage and disgust until I started to unload the groceries.

I placed the last bag in and slammed the trunk down when a hand landed on my shoulder. "You all right?" Zion asked.

"Yeah, fine," I said, a little snippy. "Can we just go?"

"Course." He nodded and went to the passenger side. I got in the driver seat and just sat there for a beat before punching the steering wheel. Why did they have to fucking show their faces? Why did she call out to me? I wished they'd stayed under the rock where they'd been living.

"Hey," Zion said, his hand dropping to my thigh. "Forget about them."

"Fuckin' motherfuckers." I shook my head. "Did you see how fuckin' spaced out they were? Probably lookin' for their next hit. Nothin' has changed for them since I left. They didn't give a flyin' fuck I was gone." I laughed humorlessly. "I'm surprised they even remembered they had a son."

"You're better off without them," Zion tried. "Hell, Boom and Wendy are your parents, not those cunts. Forget about them."

Easier said than done. But I wanted to try though. I wanted what we'd planned—an afternoon with Zion with a drink, strip poker, and some fooling around. I wanted to wipe them from my mind, but I couldn't get their image out of my head.

"Maybe if I stayed, they'd have got help," I thought aloud.

"Fuckin' bullshit." Zion tapped me in the arm. "Don't do this shit to yourself. Don't second-guess things now because they showed their fuckin' ugly mugs. They put themselves in this position. Not you. Boom got you out, and they coulda used that to wake themselves up, but they didn't. It's their choice, their mistake. Not yours." He grabbed my hand. "You're in a good place in life. Surrounded by good people. Don't let them bring you down."

Sighing, I rested my head back and nodded. "You're right." He was, and I'd fucking try to forget what just happened. They weren't worth it.

"I'm always right. You just gotta remember that."

I snorted and suddenly felt better, more relaxed, and I knew it had to do with the man next to me.

CHAPTER FOURTEEN
SAINT

I smirked at the fucking stunning man across from me. We'd given up poker when we fought too much over me, apparently, cheating. Since I was still fully clothed and Kylo was down to his boxers and socks.

Kylo glared. "Do you have a five?" he asked.

I did, but I wasn't a fair player. "Go fish."

"Bullshit, let me see your damn hand," he demanded, trying to lean over the coffee table to get to me.

Chuckling, I held them out of the way. "Now look who wants to cheat."

"Fine," he gritted between clenched teeth. I nearly had him naked. There wasn't a chance I'd give him what he wanted—which was to win—when I just had to hold out a bit longer to have him naked in front of me.

"You hard?" I asked.

"Fuck off," he clipped.

Grinning, I went on, "Right then, do you have any twos?" I didn't have a two left, I had the five he wanted, but he didn't need to know.

He smiled smugly. "Go fuckin' fish."

Shrugging, I picked up a card from the deck, and just my luck, it was a five. "I'm out."

His eyes widened, then narrowed. "Show me."

I clutched my heart. "Are you sayin' you don't trust me?"

His brow rose. "In cards, no."

"Just take it off, baby." I grinned.

He gave me the middle finger before leaning back and lifting a foot to grab his sock.

I shook my head. "I want the boxers."

"You can't tell me what piece of clothin'."

"If you remove the boxers, I'll make it worth your while." I winked.

"That should come off sleazy, so why do I find it's not?"

Chuckling, I said, "Because you like me."

Kylo stood. His thumbs hooked into the sides of his boxers, and slowly, he started to push them down. I got to see the start of his dick when we heard a key going into the front door. Kylo's eyes flared, he grabbed up a tee, but the person was already stepping through the door.

"Fuckin' knew it," Death said as he stood there staring at both of us. I hadn't moved, except to lean back against the couch.

"Yo," I said, then glanced at Kylo. "Remind me to take my keys off the brothers." I shifted back to Death. "You never know what you're gonna walk in on."

"When did this start?" he asked, crossing his arms over his chest.

"A while ago," I told him. "Want a drink?"

Kylo growled under his breath.

I grinned as Death chuckled. "Another time. You for real about this?" he asked me.

"Hell yes."

Death eyed me a little longer. "Don't fuckin' mess him around."

"Not plannin' on it."

He grunted. "Good. Have fun. I'm out."

"Later," I called.

"Yeah, ah, bye," Kylo said. When Death was gone, he turned to me. "That was weird."

I snorted. "Nah, he's just lookin' out for you."

His head jerked back. "I didn't know he…."

"Cared?"

"Well, yeah." He shook his head. "How many brothers have keys?"

"Death, State, Country, Wreck, and Quake. I didn't care who popped in, until now. I'll get the keys back, but they'll ask questions about why I want them."

"Just say you're seein' someone."

"You know Country will want to know who."

He bit his bottom lip and shrugged. "Tell him."

"Yeah?"

He straightened. "Yeah, I mean… you like me. I like you. We're gonna see this out, right?"

He sounded so unsure and adorable. Fuck me. I wanted to drag him across the coffee table and take his mouth. If both my arms were working, I would have. For now, I settled on saying, "You're right, lover, we're gonna see where this goes."

"You're certain? I'm not gonna grow boobs or a pussy, so you're shit outta luck in that area."

I threw my head back and laughed. Damn, he was a fool. I knew that. Of fucking course I knew that. I liked what he had for me. Shit, I wasn't even pushing for sex between us because I enjoyed the handies and blow jobs. Hell, I even liked fondling his dick.

Never thought it'd be something I'd think—how I loved his dick —but I did.

Smiling, I shook my head. "Like you exactly the way you are, Kylo."

He nodded. "Okay. All right. Then yeah, we're doin' this." He nodded again. "There, it's out in the open. We're datin'." Even though he'd said it, he still looked at me to make sure it was certain.

"We are. Now get your ass over here and kiss me," I ordered.

"How about you come to me?" He crossed his arms over his

chest.

I stood, walked around the coffee table, tagged the back of his head, and tugged him into me where he had to brace his hands on my stomach.

"Like you, lover," I told him, my tone throatier than usual.

His hands shifted down to dip under my tee and slide up, running them over my skin, causing me to shiver just from his touch. "Like you too, Zion."

I kissed the corner of his mouth. "Glad to hear it, lover." With another kissed pressed into the corner of his mouth, I felt him smile. I pulled back and asked, "What?"

"I just can't fuckin' believe this is where I am with you."

I cocked my head to the side. "What do you mean?"

His arms curled around my waist and he dropped his forehead to my shoulder. "I'm in your house, arms, and it seems like you enjoy my touch." I hummed under my breath and waited for more. He shook his head and snorted. "I had the biggest crush on you when I first started comin' around the compound more." He lifted his head, his cheeks tinted pink while I stilled from shock.

"Serious?"

"Fuck yeah, always thought you were hot. But I pushed it away because it was stupid. You were straight."

"Well, fuck. I'd always thought you were good-lookin', but my eyes didn't open until you were cocky and braggin' about how good you were at giving head. I had to test it out. I wanted your mouth on me so damn bad."

His hands cupped my ass and he pulled me into him where I felt his hardness, which matched mine. "And I wanted to suck you off so damn bad. Glad you were stubborn."

I grinned. "So am I."

We both leaned into each other. The kiss started out sweet and exploring, but when Kylo gripped my ass tightly, it grew into something hotter and heavier. I sucked on his tongue and then nibbled on his bottom lip, dragging out a low moan from his lips.

"Bedroom, now," he ordered.

"Soon," I said, then kissed him again until Kylo picked me up like I was some damsel, which I didn't mind too much, and carried me into my bedroom. He set me on my feet. "That was damn hot," I told him.

"Shut up. It was not," he said as he helped me out of my tee.

"It damn was," I demanded. He still didn't see how he got me going. It wasn't just his looks, but his actions, his timidness, his passion, his aggression. Everything.

He rolled his eyes, but then they heated when he undid my jeans and pushed them down my legs. I flicked them off to the side and he bent, removing my socks like he didn't care he was helping me disrobe. Who wouldn't really when I was hot myself? I wasn't talking out of my ass either. I knew I was attractive, or how else did I bag a lot of women? And now a man. Just the one man. I couldn't see myself with any other.

He straightened, hooked his fingers in my boxers, and forced them down. I stepped out and cocked a brow at him. "Now what?"

"Gonna make you feel good," he said, gently pushing me back onto the bed, and I noticed he still had his underwear on.

"You already do," I said as I sat on the edge and scooted back using my good arm. "You gonna get naked too?"

"Soon, and don't say shit like I already do."

"Why?"

Leaning in, he kissed my leg and softly admitted, "I like it too much."

"I'm glad you do because I mean it."

He kissed my thigh, my hip, and just above my hard cock. "You trust me?"

"Yes. Always."

He hummed under his breath before getting off the bed and walking to my bedside table where the lube lay. He took it out and threw it down to the bed before going back to between my legs.

"What're you thinkin'?"

He smirked. "You'll see. Just lay back and relax." When I didn't move, he added, "Please."

Giving in, I rested back on the bed and closed my eyes, feeling Kylo kissing, nipping, and sucking on my skin around my dick. Fuck, it was driving me crazy. He knew I needed his mouth on my dick, but he wasn't giving it.

"Kylo," I grumbled.

"Patience," he reprimanded. Slowly, he licked all the way up to my nipple, where he bit down. "Fuckin' love your body."

"And it loves you back."

"Spread your legs a bit more," he uttered against my skin. I did, and he shifted up a little more between me.

Finally, his hand wound around my erection. Somehow, he'd already had the strawberry-flavored lube in his palm, which had him easily gliding his hand up and down on it.

"Christ," I muttered, slamming my eyes closed. How did Kylo make me feel more than I had with a woman just from him touching me? I didn't know, but I loved it.

He kissed down my stomach, swirled his tongue around my belly button, and that was when I first felt his other hand between my legs. I tensed a little until he kissed his way up my body and took my mouth with his. I wished my arm didn't hurt like a bitch when I moved it, because I would have grabbed him and dragged him against me. Instead, I settled for running my hand up and down his side.

A finger slid over my asshole. I paused until it stayed where it was, and Kylo distracted me with more kissing. The finger gently rubbed around my hole, and I started getting into it more. In fact, I didn't mind the feel of it at all. Spreading my legs wider, I cupped the back of Kylo's head and held onto him, pouring everything I felt into the heated kiss.

I only broke it when I pushed my head back into the mattress and cursed, "Fuckin' hell." Kylo had inserted his finger inside me and touched something that sent a shockwave through my body.

Blinking dazedly, I asked, "What was that?"

Kylo grinned down at me. "Your prostate." He glided his finger over it again, and my whole body tightened in pleasure.

"Fuck me," I panted, slamming my eyes closed to let this new, and fucking awesome, sensation take over. I ground my feet into the bed while Kylo drove me fucking wild. "Jesus," I muttered.

Already, the bite of release approached. I didn't want it though. I wanted to bask in the damn good feeling Kylo was showing me.

"You like that?" Kylo asked.

"Fuck yes," I groaned.

"Christ, Zion, you look so good lettin' me play. So fuckin' good."

"It feels damn good."

He chuckled low. "That it does."

I clenched my teeth and hissed out a breath when he brushed over it again and again. "Close," I managed to get out. How in the fuck was I close? It wasn't something to ponder over though, not when— "Ah, fuck," I yelled as the first drop of cum shot out. I rocked down on his finger as I kept coming all over my stomach.

"Yeah, Zion, so good," Kylo whispered.

Once I'd stopped and settled, Kylo removed his finger, and I blinked lazily up at him. He grabbed a tee from the floor, which looked a lot like mine, but I didn't care, and cleaned up my gut and his hand.

He smirked when he saw me watching him. "Now you know why I use a damn dildo."

Laughter burst out of me unexpectedly. "Not sure I'm ready for that."

His head jerked back in shock. "You'd want to try?"

Grinning, I asked, "You were here a few seconds ago when I blew a load from ass play?"

He chuckled. "I was here."

"Then you'll get why I'd be more than willin' to do it again." I grinned.

He leaned over me. "You're... pretty awesome, Zion."

Reaching up, I ran a finger over his lips and shook my head. "Nah, lover, it's you who's awesome."

He screwed his nose up as if he didn't agree, but I knew for certain it was true. No one else would get me interested in them like I was with Kylo. No one else had captured my attention and held it, made me want more, than Kylo.

He was special.

And he was mine.

I'd make sure I did everything in my power to keep it that way.

"Stop thinkin' so hard. You'll blow a gasket," Kylo teased before resting on me gently and taking my lips in a sweet-tasting kiss.

He lifted off me after a final peck and said, "Gonna hit the bathroom. Be back."

I grabbed his hand. "Don't think I've forgotten about you." As soon as I got the energy back after seeing stars from coming so hard, I'd have my mouth around his dick, showing him how much I loved pleasing him.

He smiled softly, dipped down, and kissed me quickly before brushing his lips against my ear, where he said, "Already came, sweetheart. Watchin' you had me jizzin' in my boxers like a thirteen-year-old seeing a pair of tits for the first time."

My eyes flashed wide. When he stood, he caught my cocky grin and rolled his eyes.

"Now that is fuckin' hot, lover."

"What, that I can't control myself when I see you gettin' off on me finger fuckin' you?"

"Hell yes." I nodded.

He snorted. "You're somethin' else."

I winked. "You know it. Hurry the hell up. I need some damn snuggles from my man." His steps faltered a little, but his eyes warmed and he nodded.

He liked me claiming him as my man, and I enjoyed knowing I did that for him, but I also felt it was right in my head and heart.

He was my man.

CHAPTER FIFTEEN
KYLO

Walking into the house, I was headed for my bedroom when Boom called my name. "Comin'," I yelled back. I dumped my bag with my extra clothes I carried around since, in the last two weeks, I happened to stay a lot at Zion's. He'd tried to get me to leave my shit there, even cleaned out a drawer for me, but it felt like too much too soon. I gave in on the toothbrush, but that was it.

I had to be smart about some things. He'd already won on us dating. Although I wanted it probably more than him, living together was a full commitment we weren't ready for.

Not that Zion agreed.

But I was doing this for us. We couldn't go right to living out of each other's pockets, maybe in another month or two, but not after nearly two months together.

As I walked toward the kitchen, where I knew Boom would be since I could hear Wendy clattering around in there and he was never far from her, my phone chimed. I pulled it free and was surprised when I saw West's name on there.

West: Do you have time later for a chat?

Weird he was coming to me and not Lucas as they were best

friends. Yet, West and I had become friends. I just didn't think we were as close as what those two were, or what I was with Lucas.

Me: Sure. When and where?

He said a name of a coffeehouse and a time. I told him I'd be there and put the phone back in my pocket by the time I walked into the kitchen.

"Hey," I said, making my way up to Wendy and kissing her on the cheek.

"Hey, honey, you want some lunch?"

"No thanks, I'm heading out again shortly to meet with someone." I faced Boom as I leaned against the counter. "What's up, Boom?"

"Where you been?" he asked, then took a sip of his coffee.

"Boom," Wendy warned.

"What's this?" I asked, looking between them.

"Wendy reckons I shouldn't ask you about your love life, but it's obvious you're with someone. You hardly spend nights here anymore. When we gonna meet her… or him?"

Shit.

What could I say? We'd told Country what was happening between us, well, Zion did, and Country was happy that we were happy, but was it too soon to tell other people? I liked our bubble of bliss we had going on. But Boom and Wendy were my family. Zion's parents knew, so they should, right?

"One second," I told him, taking my phone out again and shooting a text off to Zion.

Me: Boom wants to know who I've got hiding.

Zion: Up to you, but I don't care if they know.

Just like that, he didn't care about coming out, even when this was new for him, being with a guy.

Me: Okay, thanks. Talk soon!

Zion: Better, already missing you.

Fuck, the things he said got me mushy inside. I'd never been fucking mushy. The prick. Looking up, I realized I was smiling; so were Boom and Wendy.

"Whoever it is, we can see the person makes you happy," Wendy said.

"Yeah, he does."

"He?" Boom questioned. "Who is it? And if you say Lucas, be prepared for Wreck to kill you."

I snorted. "Definitely not Lucas… but this person's in the same family."

Boom choked on his sip of coffee. "Saint?"

"What?" Wendy whispered.

"Zion and I have been seein' each other for nearly two months now."

Boom dropped his mug to the counter. "Saint? The fucker is a player. I swear to Christ, if he's fuckin' with you, I'll end him myself." He stood, grabbed his keys, and went to move out of the room.

"Boom, wait, Jesus. I'm not sayin' I don't love that you care, but this is happenin', and it's real." Fuck, I hoped it was…. No, it was. Zion was being real with me.

Boom ground his jaws together. Wendy walked over and put a hand on his chest. "I'm still havin' a word with him," Boom said.

I sighed. "Boom."

"Honey," Wendy started. "You're our kid. We're going to want to take care of you no matter how old you get. Even I heard of Saint's prowess when it came to women. What's the harm if Boom has a word with him?"

When she put it like that, I couldn't exactly tell them no. "Fine." Especially since I didn't think anything could scare Zion off. He'd been the one to chase me, to want me. When I'd been scared, it was all Zion going full force into this with me, not leaving me to cling to my fear about us together.

"Right then," Boom said, then nodded. "We care about you, kid."

Smiling, I rolled my eyes. "Not a kid, Boom."

"Know that, but you always will be to us."

Fucking hell, I loved them. They'd been the best people in my life.

"Love you guys. You know that, right? I don't say it enough, but I do. Wouldn't have lived if it wasn't for you guys."

Wendy's bottom lip wobbled. Boom tucked her in close as he cleared his throat. "Yeah, well, you know you got our love. Now enough of this shit." He kissed Wendy's temple. "I'll be back." He pointed to me. "I won't shed any of his blood if you help me in a couple of weeks to paint the garage."

Grinning, I said, "You got it, Boom."

I WAS ALREADY SITTING at a table when West walked through the door. He looked good, but he always did. Not that I'd ever go there. Like Lucas, I knew West and I would be better as friends.

West smiled when he saw me and waded through the tables. "Hey, thanks for meeting me," he said, pulling out the chair opposite me and sitting down.

"No problem." I nodded toward the coffee. "Got it for you, plus the muffin." I pushed the plate with the chocolate one on it closer to him, while I pulled my blueberry one in.

"Thanks, surprised you remembered."

I shrugged. "Can't forget how you went on and on about chocolate muffins."

He snorted. "I didn't go on and on—Jesus, this tastes amazing," he mumbled around a mouthful. Chuckling, I raised a brow, and West gave me a glare.

"Anyway, what's been happenin'?"

He stared down at his muffin before looking over my shoulder, then the other, and when he shrugged, he said, "Nothing much."

"West, you didn't call me here for small talk. We're friends, right?" He nodded. "Then you should know whatever you say, I'll keep it to myself."

He let out a breath. "How are you finding working at… you know?"

"Things have been good. Are you findin' it hard?"

"No… well, sort of, but…." He growled under his breath and ripped apart the muffin a little more.

"What'd the muffin do to you?" I asked.

He stilled, dropped the crumbs, and brushed his hands together before leaning back in his seat. Then he was leaning forward and blurted, "I'm in trouble."

"What?" I clipped. "How?"

He shook his head. "Not the type you think…. Fuck, Kylo, I think I like a client."

Oh fuck.

"I presume this person is a guy?"

"Yes." He nodded and got a far-off look with dreamy eyes. Shit it all out. He was lovesick for a client. This wasn't good unless the client felt something for him.

"Do you think this guy could… I don't know, like you back?"

He bit his bottom lip and shrugged.

Shit.

I winced and scrubbed a hand over my face. "West, I don't know if this is good."

He dropped his head and groaned, running a hand through his hair. "I know. But I can't stop thinking about him."

"What are you gonna do?"

"That's the thing. I don't know." He threw his hands up. "Do I stop going there? Do I get Saint or Country or State to get him someone else? Do I keep going and try to stop my feelings?" His eyes landed on me. "You need to tell me what to do. I have too much going on. I don't need this extra stress in my life, and all because I couldn't stop getting feelings for a client. Jesus, I'm pathetic."

Leaning across, I punched him in the arm.

"What was that for?"

"To stop you from freakin' out."

"It worked because all I want to do now is punch you back."

I nodded. "Good. Now, you're not pathetic. I gave Saint a blow job on the first night, and now we're seein' each other."

I could have picked a better time to say that, like when West hadn't taken a large gulp of his coffee since he sprayed it all over the table, and a few drops landed on me.

He coughed and choked, even slapped the table. We got the attention of others around us. I waved it off and said, "He's fine."

West pounded his fist against his chest. "You what?" he rasped.

I smirked. "Yeah, you heard. So, in a way, I know what you mean. I tried to stay away from him because I thought he was as straight as they came, but he was persistent. What I'm gettin' at is that it worked out for me. But Saint wasn't a client. What vibes do you get from this guy?"

"Mixed. I know he enjoys my company, but we haven't even kissed or… done anything else. He pays for my time to come and just"—he shrugged—"hang out with him. Yet, I think he's interested. There've been moments. Tell me what I should do."

"I can't tell you that, West."

He sighed. "I was afraid you'd say that. I'd quit, but I need this job, and they haven't been pushing me into sleeping with a client. I only go on dates, so it's a good job to have."

"I haven't been pushed either, but I'm sure that has somethin' to do with Saint and us being friends with Lucas."

He gave me a small smile. "At least there's that. But do I give up this client who I make money off because of my feelings?"

"How often do you see this guy?"

"Every second weekend. Do you think they could get me another client? And would you take him on since I know you're not sleeping with anyone either and you're with Saint, which I still can't believe."

I winced. "Not sure Saint would like me takin' on a male client. All I've had are females."

Hell, there I went worried about what Zion would think, but I knew deep down I'd never want him pissed over anything, and if I did have men as clients, I was sure that'd send him into a mood.

"What about one of the other guys?" I suggested.

West licked his lips as he thought about it. "Maybe." But I could already tell he wasn't a fan of the thought since the other recruits were ones who'd been sexual with their clients.

"I'm not much help. But the main point is that if you could walk away from this guy, would you be okay with it? Is there a chance of somethin' with him?"

He frowned. "I don't think there is." He looked away and blinked rapidly. "He's very closed off. I don't think he's out, and I'm being stupid for even thinking about something with him." He sat back, deflated.

"Then I think you have your answer. For your sake, it's probably best to walk away. Get the bosses to switch you out."

He nodded as he ground his teeth together. "You're right. I hate it, but you're right. Thank you for listening and talking this out with me."

"West, it's what friends do."

"Speaking of friends, I'd prefer it if Lucas doesn't know about this. It isn't that I don't trust him, but he's in his own happy bubble of bliss, and I don't want to drag him down with any of my troubles."

"I won't say anything because I agree, which is why Saint and I haven't said anythin' to anyone really. Well, except a few people."

West nodded. Though, he looked like he was far away with other thoughts.

"Hey," I started. When I had his eyes, I went on, "Is there somethin' else botherin' you?"

He rubbed the back of his neck and snorted. "What isn't these days?"

"Anythin' I can help with?"

He grinned. "Want to sit in on my classes and take my tests, so I don't fail and lose my scholarship? But then there's med school, which will be just as busy and another reason I need to keep this job, because they don't care about my hours. But if anyone finds out I work there, it could destroy my career. I also need to get out of my unit, find a place, so I don't have to go home and be suffocated by my parents. They don't know I'm gay. Lucas thinks they're all supportive and shit, but...." He shook his head. "I'm rambling. Forget it. I'll be fine." He laughed, but it wasn't a real one. "I think I just need sleep."

"Not sure I can help with much of any of that. But what about Lucas's offer of you movin' in with them? I'm sure they'd be cheaper than wherever you are, and then you could save a little or even quit at P and P for a normal job if it worries you that much."

He nodded. "Yeah, I might just have to, but I have a little time to work things out."

"How little is little?"

"About the moving situation, probably a week." He smirked.

"West, Lucas's place is huge. I'm pretty sure he was serious when he said you guys wouldn't see each other. There's nothin' wrong with leanin' on friends."

His brows rose. "You ever done it?"

"That's the thing. I've never really had people I could call friends until you and Lucas. Yeah, I have Boom, Wendy, and the brothers, but that's all different. They're more like family. I know my brothers would help me out in a pinch and would listen to me if needed. But ever since Lucas and you came into my life, I've just known it's been different between us. We're like... shit, the three bi or gay amigos."

West laughed, and it was good to see. I wondered if there was another way I could help him out. I was sure it'd be healthier for him to get out of the job he was in. A thought occurred to me. I'd have to find out more information before I could voice it with West, but it could be good for him in the end.

It wasn't until West and I parted ways that I made a call.

"Yo, Gun, what's happenin'?" Death answered. The awkward

stage had gone when he'd walked in on Zion and me half naked, hard, and ready to play. No one couldn't be at ease around Death; he was just that type of guy.

The brothers had taken it in stride and started to call me Gun right away after Country had patched me in. It was good, made me feel complete within the club and like I belonged more than I had within the brothers. It'd also been the same day where we'd punished the motherfucking cunt Steve. Along with the gunshot wound in his foot, he had a broken hand, a busted-up face, and a threat that if he ever stepped out of line with another woman in his life, he'd be dead. Death had made sure to set up surveillance on him. No one got away with shit that involved the club in any way. People would learn that eventually.

"Just got a question for you, brother."

"Hit me," Death stated.

"You got any openins' in the surveillance room for two people?"

He started to chuckle. "I'm guessin' one is you. What, Saint doesn't like his man around others?"

"He hasn't said shit, but I'd be more comfortable in a different situation." It wasn't that I hated working at the Polished Pussies and Penises club. I did like it. I enjoyed making my clients happy for the hours I was with them. But lately, I'd been feeling like shit going out on dates, even when it was work, without Zion there. It felt like, in a way, I was stepping out on him.

Jesus, I was mad for the guy.

"Who's the other?" Death asked, bringing me out of my thoughts.

"West."

He hummed under his breath. "Leave it with me."

"Will do, brother," I said and ended the call. If this worked out, the money might not be the same, but I heard it was still good. It could work out for West and me. Fuck, I hoped so.

CHAPTER SIXTEEN
SAINT

*S*miling, I sat with my back against the headboard of my bed and Kylo between my spread legs while he rested against my chest and we watched some fucking show Kylo liked about werewolves. I'd just finished telling him about Boom's phone call.

Kylo snorted. He tilted his head so he could look up at me. "He seriously threatened to cut off your balls and said even though I probably like them?"

"Yep," I replied.

"Jesus." Kylo shook his head and shifted to watch his show again. I curled my arms around his shoulders tighter. It was moments like these I loved—just the quiet times where we could chill, talk, and just be with each other.

"Well?" I asked.

"Well what?" Kylo questioned.

"Do you like my balls?"

He snorted out a laugh. "Yeah, Zion. I like them enough that I want to keep them on your body, so you better not piss me off or hurt me, or I'll sic Boom onto you."

Slowly, I ran a hand down his chest and stomach, tracing my

fingers over his skin. He twitched. "You know I'll never intentionally hurt you."

"I know," he said, threading our fingers together and holding them against his stomach. "The same goes for me."

"I like what we have, Kylo. A damn lot, and I'd do anything to keep what we have. Never have I wanted someone to stay by my side as much as I do you."

He brought our hands up and kissed my knuckles. "It blows my damn mind I am where I am with you. Never thought it'd happen, but I'm fuckin' lucky and happy to have you as mine."

Christ, my chest expanded and filled with warmth.

"I'm the lucky one, but I'll let you say that."

He laughed. "Gee, thanks."

I grinned and kissed his shoulder. "No problem."

"Do you feel like you wanna tell the brothers? Lucas?"

"Yeah, soon I reckon that's where it should go. I don't wanna hide what we have."

"Me either, but could we wait just a little longer?"

"Anything you want, baby."

He took a breath and then said, "I caught up with West today."

"Yeah?"

"Yeah, he's in a bind, not sure what to do, but we talked it out, and I think he now knows."

"What?"

"That he needs to get out of Polished P and P."

"Why? Doesn't he like it, or does he have a problem with a client? If a client's fuckin' with him, he should come to me, State, Wreck, or Country."

"It's nothin' like that. Shit, I'm not even sure if I should have said anything to you."

"Kylo, you know I won't say anythin' to anyone unless I think it's necessary."

"I know. I also know that we're together and this sort of stuff happens."

"What, us talkin'?" I asked in a light tone. His elbow hit my ribs. "Ouch, Jesus, you have a pointy elbow."

"Yeah, well, I'll use it again if you annoy me. I mean that we're together. We share shit before anyone else. So, I'm gonna tell you what's goin' on."

Dipping down, I kissed his shoulder. It'd been fucking forever since I'd had a relationship. I think the last one was back in high school, but this one right here meant more to me than that, and more than any other woman I'd been with. I wanted to have him at my side as much as I could.

It sounded a lot like love to me. I wasn't ready to spout poetry or say the words that meant so fucking much, but I recognized what I was feeling, and it sat right with me.

"All right," he started with a nod. "West has a thing for a client."

Fuck. That couldn't be good.

"Shit, what's he gonna do?"

"Since he's pretty sure the client only wants him for company and nothin' more, he's lookin' at gettin' one of you to switch him out."

"Probably for the best. All clients we deal with are mainly after a warm hole to slide into. Then there's the ones who do just want company or to show off some arm candy without any complications."

"I agree, which is why I hinted it would be good to get away from this client while he could. However, I also had an idea. I spoke to Death this afternoon because West was sayin' he's worried if his current employment ever got out later in his years while he's a doctor, it wouldn't be good. I asked Death if he had anythin' goin' in the surveillance room. The hours could be good for him to work around other things."

"Yeah, good thinkin'. Death said somethin' the other day about openin' up another business, which could lead to more jobs, but he didn't say what type of business. Some of the guys from the security agency could want a change if things go ahead."

"Huh, didn't know that, and you don't have a clue what type of business?"

"Nope, he rambled on about somethin' then went on about somethin' else in the next breath. I'm sure we'll find out soon."

His fingers ran over my hand. "Gonna ask you somethin' and want you to be honest about it."

"You got it."

"What do you think when I go out on a job?"

I stilled. He wanted me to be honest, but I wasn't really sure of my answer because I was half and half over it.

"Kylo…," I whined and dropped my head back against the headboard.

"Zion, tell me, please."

"Fuck, all right. I understand why you're doin' what you're doin' to get on your own two feet and have somethin' behind you."

"But?"

"To start with, when we'd first started out, I wasn't worried about it. Now, I hate the fuckin' thought of someone else touchin' you, even when it's as innocent as hand-holdin'. But that's me bein' jealous, and it's not fair to you. Which is why I probably should have shut my damn mouth because I don't want you to feel guilty over it."

He sat up and got to his knees to face me. "That's the thing. Lately I feel shitty for goin' out there with them. Which is why I also asked Death about a job."

"You shittin' me?"

He grinned but rolled his eyes. "No. I mean, like West I'll have to do it until we can get somethin' figured out, and this is all dependin' on Death having some openin's."

Reaching out, I ran a hand up his thigh. "You wantin' to do that for us means a fuckin' lot. Surprised the hell outta me you already got the ball rollin'. But it's good."

Yeah, this was fuckin' love between us, and I couldn't wait to see how much it grew with time.

"You gonna show me how good you think it is?" His cocky arch of a brow got my dick jerking.

"Yeah, lover, I'll show you real good." Un-fucking-fortunately, my phone rang. "Shit."

Kylo reached for my cell, handing it over, saying, "Country."

"Hey, Prez, what's happenin'?"

"How's the arm, Saint?"

"Good, Prez. Healing nicely."

"Great to hear. You able to head to Polished? Know it's my night on, but I gotta go deal with somethin'. State and Wreck ain't answerin'. Need a manager here. Sorry, brother."

Fuck it all.

"No problem, Country, I'll be there in ten."

"Thanks, and tell Gun sorry for draggin' you away from him."

Chuckling, I said, "Will do." I ended the call and told Kylo, "Country's sorry for takin' me away from you, but I gotta head into Polished to take his shift. He's got somethin' on."

"I'll come with you," he said, climbing off the bed.

Standing, I grabbed his arm and pulled him into me. "Stay. Rest. You'll be bored shitless if you did come."

"Or I could give you head under the desk?" he offered with a cheeky grin.

Laughing, I shook my head. "Another time." I kissed his nose, which he screwed up. "No use both of us bein' tired. Get some sleep. You'll need energy when I get home."

"You'd better be worked up and ready to rock then."

"Oh, I fuckin' will be, knowin' you're here in our bed waitin' for me."

His hand cupped the back of my neck and he drew me in for a heavy and hot kiss that left me breathless and wanting more.

When he stepped away and dove on the bed again, I pointed at my junk and said, "See what you fuckin' do with one kiss?"

He chuckled and grabbed his own erection. "Know the feelin'." He sobered and ordered, "Be safe."

Bending, I gave him a quick kiss. "Always." I quickly got dressed and out of there before Kylo's magic had me saying, "Screw it all," and jumping back in bed with him like I wanted to.

By the time I got to Polished, I was freezing my ass off. The fucking heater in the Jeep decided to kick the bucket on one of the coldest nights. I pulled my jacket around me more as I made my way into Polished. I couldn't help but feel unsettled. I really didn't want to be here and wished I was back with Kylo. I knew I was damn lovesick, but usually I could handle a few hours away from the guy. Tonight was different, and I didn't understand it.

Me: You good there?

Kylo: Yep, you made it all right?

Me: Yeah, except for the heater in the Jeep taking a hike.

Kylo: I'll take a look at it tomorrow.

Me: Thanks, now rest up, lover.

Kylo: Already looking forward to seeing you.

Me: Same.

Placing my phone on my desk, I sat when a knock came to the door. "Enter," I called.

West stepped in. "Hey, ah, I thought Country was on tonight?"

"He had to step out. What's up?"

He glanced around everywhere but at me, then cleared his throat and said to the floor, "Right… ah, my regular, Mr. Hail?" I hummed under my breath, so he knew he had my attention since he wasn't looking at me still. "Well, is there any chance I could be switched out with someone else?"

Since I had to pretend Kylo hadn't said anything, I had to ask, "Has he done somethin'?"

His eyes snapped to me. "No, no, nothing like that. It's just…" He sighed and scrubbed a hand over his face. "I like him. I didn't mean to get feelings, but I did and don't think it's perfect for me to continue because it could lead to me hurting in the end, and if I prevent that now, it would be better in the long run." He started pacing. "Shit, I didn't mean to get feelings and don't know why I have. He's never done anything indicating that he likes me, but I just like being around him. Even when he doesn't talk so much." He groaned. "Jesus, I'm fucking useless."

"West," I called. He stopped and faced me. "It's fine. I'll look into it. Besides, you've got your other regular customers to keep you going." I glanced down at the roster Country must have left on my desk. "Are you okay to see him tonight?"

His eyes widened. "I don't usually have him. We're set for every second weekend, and that would be next weekend. Shit, what do I do? I can't leave him in the lurch and not go, and then if I do go, I could end up rambling." He growled at himself. "I'm not usually like this. He sends me into a ranting fool because he confuses me." He leaned into the desk and whispered, "I don't even think he's really gay. Was there a mistake in the office end? Did he ask for a woman to start with and then I showed?"

"No mistake and, West, how about I see if I have someone else available for him tonight?"

He sighed and nodded. "It's probably a good idea."

"All right, I'll call him and tell him of the change and see if he wants someone else. Take a break. Then you have your other client at eleven who wants arm candy at a club."

"Thanks, Saint. I really appreciate it."

"No problem, West. Our employees come first, always."

As soon as he was gone, I brought up Mr. Hail's details. The details Death had found on him were that he was a businessman who owned a few casinos in Vegas. It was obvious he was a private person from the lack of details we had on him, and West had been our first employee assigned to him. Since I knew he'd respected the boundaries we had for West, meaning no sex in any form, I couldn't find a fault in him.

Pressing in his number on the office phone, I waited for him to answer. I checked the time West and he usually caught up. Other than the first time, which was earlier, the rest had been set for late in the night—midnight, in fact. At least I had a couple of hours to find him someone else if he wanted.

"*Da*," he answered in Russian. I only knew it was Russian from a show I'd seen.

"Mr. Hail, this is Saint, co-owner from Polished. Unfortunately, Ben is no longer available. Would you like to reschedule with someone else?"

There was a pause, and then he asked, "Is he good?"

"He is." I wasn't going to give him more than I needed.

"Will he be available for next weekend as usual?" His accent was thick where *will* sounded like vill.

"Unfortunately, no, sorry. If you go to our website, we have more men online for you to view. I'll just have to give you the password to access them." Which I would since we'd already looked into him.

"*Net*," he clipped in Russian. "I would prefer Ben. Is he working with your company still?"

Fuck, it didn't seem like this guy wanted to give up West, which had me thinking maybe the attraction had been two way and not just on West's side.

"He does, for now, but the hours he'd been doin' aren't suitin' him any longer."

"I'll take any hour he has available."

"I'm sorry, but that won't be possible. He's already been booked out for the next month with his new hours." I was talking out of my ass and hoping this guy would buy it.

"Will he be sleeping with these other clients?" he bit out.

"It's no business of yours what my employee does," I told him with a hardness to my voice.

"Fine. Give me the access code and I'll take a look, then get back to you."

I passed on the code, since I couldn't not, even though I didn't fucking like his attitude. We ended the call, and I sat back in the seat, staring at the phone. It wouldn't be bad if I had Death look further into Mr. Hail. I made a note of it before Erica walked into the office and I gave her the details for her night.

As the hours dragged by, I couldn't help but feel off, the urge to call Kylo riding me hard. My gut had been twisted since I got here. I'd just reached for my phone when my door crashed open.

Torch stood there, panting, "Get to the hospital. Gun's hurt."

I stood and grabbed my things as fear had my blood rushing through me. My chest ached like a bitch. "What the fuck happened?" I demanded, making my way out.

Torch followed me to the doors. "Just get there, brother. Drive safe."

Fuck, fuck, fuck, why wouldn't he say? Did it mean it wasn't good? I couldn't think of it now. I had to get to the hospital and find out what the fuck was going on. Then, and only when I knew Kylo was okay, could I let myself think and feel.

CHAPTER SEVENTEEN
KYLO

Already I missed him, and he hadn't even been gone long. What was good was that Zion seemed to be having the same problem since it was only moments ago he'd messaged me from the club. The show I usually loved just wasn't keeping my attention. Maybe sleep was what I needed, and then the time would go faster for when Zion got home.

Fuck me sideways. I sounded like a lovesick fool.

But I couldn't help it because Zion was… hell, everything I'd ever wanted to have in a relationship. He made me smile, gave me those stupid yet kickass feelings in the gut, and my heart beat faster every time he was near, and I hadn't seen him in a while.

Was it too soon to call it love?

Fuck it.

I was in love with Zion Storey.

He was mine.

Mine.

Just thinking it brought a smile to my face.

Laughing at myself, I climbed off the bed and made my way into the kitchen. Maybe the fluttering in my gut was hunger and not from thinking of Zion. Who was I kidding? It was Zion. Still, while I was there, I grabbed a glass and filled it with water. Leaning my ass against the counter, I looked around the place.

I'd felt more at home here as each day passed. I knew Zion would have me move in if he had a choice, but it still scared me we were moving too fast and that it'd crash down in the end.

I didn't want it to end.

Placing the glass down on the sink, I started toward the bedroom when there was a knock on the front door. It was nearing eleven at night. Who would come to Zion's this late? I quickly grabbed a tee off the floor and went to answer. Only when I unlocked the door, it was pushed open from the outside, causing me to stumble back. Two figures entered; one hit me in the jaw, knocking me sideways from the impact.

Shaking my head, I took the person to the ground in a tackle. He let out a huff. I straddled his waist and laid a fist into his face. It was on the second hit when I recognized who it was.

Henry.

Motherfucking Henry.

My so-called father.

"Get off him" was screamed, and something smashed into my side, knocking me off Henry.

"What the fuck? What the fuck?" I shouted up at Samantha, who held a baseball bat in her hands.

Henry sat and pulled something out from behind him.

A gun.

Fuck.

My pulse was beating a million miles an hour, but it kicked up even more and sent my gut to my feet.

Slowly, I stood as Henry did.

"What do you want?" I asked, looking right at Henry. Both looked strung out, their eyes wild, their clothes tattered and torn. Samantha kept twitching her head to the side, then up and down. Henry shifted from one foot to the other and scratched at his thigh with his free hand. The one that held the gun shook, but in his state, I worried he'd fire it if I moved an inch.

"Been following you. Know where you're working. You got money, boy, and it's time you gave us some."

You have got to be fucking shitting me.

"Are you serious right now? You think I fuckin' owe you or somethin'?"

"You wouldn't be here if it wasn't for us," Samantha said in a quiet tone as she scratched at her neck.

"Yeah, she's right, you wouldn't." He waved the gun around in the air, still shifting from one foot to the other. "You wouldn't be where you are either. Bringing in money for selling yourself. Hooking up with a fucking man, you faggot. You make me sick to think you came from us, but like your momma said, you wouldn't be here without us, so you owe us, and we want it paid in money before it ends in blood."

They were threatening me.

My own parents were threatening me.

Not only that, they threatened all I'd built in my life. In a second, they could take away everything with a bullet. I couldn't let it happen. I was happy, in love, and I wanted a future with Zion at my side, yet they thought they could take that away in blood if I didn't give them money?

"You think I carry a heap of money around with me?" I asked the stupid motherfuckers.

Samantha swung the bat back and forth in front of her. "Take us to get it," she said with a giggle. She was either high or coming down from one. I expected they needed the money for more, so they thought up this fucked-up plan. "Take us, and then we'll let you walk away and never bother you again."

Bull-fucking-shit.

If they got away with it this time, they would come back again and again.

It wasn't happening.

But how did I stop it?

"No," Henry snarled. He kicked at the ground and looked around. "He ain't going anywhere." It was the grin that put dread in my veins as his eyes landed back on me. It was then I heard footsteps on the front porch. Since the door was still open, two other men stepped into the room.

"Henry, what's this? Henry, no, we talked about this," Samantha said. Her eyes were wide with horror. She stumbled over to Henry and grabbed his arm, but he shook her off.

I backed up when the guys started my way. "What's goin' on?" I demanded.

"You'll give us your PIN to your account and your bank card, or things will get messy," Henry said with a gleam in his eyes before he started cackling like a lunatic.

"Stop, no stop," Samantha yelled. She stepped forward, then back, then forward again. Her mind couldn't make up what she wanted to do. "Don't do this. Don't." Finally, she moved in front of me and tried to push the men back.

"Sammy, get the fuck outta the way," Henry growled.

"No." She stomped her foot and dropped the bat to put her hands on her hips, but she kept rolling her head from side to side. "We talked about this. Our plan was to get him to the bank, get money, and leave him alone. The plan was working. Why would you do this? We planned this. You got Country out of there with a house fire so his guy had to go to work and we could get in here. We planned this," she shouted again.

So that was how they knew Zion had left. I didn't think they'd be smart enough in the first place or fucking sober enough, but I was wrong.

"Plans change. I knew this fucker wouldn't just walk out the door with us," Henry said, scratching his arm with the gun.

"I won't let this happen," Samantha screeched, rocking back and forth on her feet.

Henry snorted. His eyes darkened as he smiled. "Like you have a choice. Now move, bitch."

"Move, Samantha," I said softly. She was a shit mother, but she proved she had a small amount of feelings for me trying to stop this shit.

She shook her head over and over and then stilled to yell, "No, I won't. I'm not moving. You said he'd be roughed up a bit not—"

The gun fired. I dove for the ground, and in the next blink, I saw Samantha's body on the floor with a hole in her head.

A boot connected with my gut hard. I coughed out a breath, but I couldn't look away from the body.

From my mother.

He shot her.

Shot his wife.

"Why?" I asked harshly.

Henry laughed. He bounced up and down as if happy he'd just killed her. "It's my way. *My* way. I was sick of her bitching and whining. Now I'll get what I want and won't have to listen to her."

I got to my knees, with three of them standing around me after one of the guys dragged Samantha's lifeless body out of the way. "She was your wife." White-hot fury burned me inside.

He chuckled. "You stupid little faggot. I only put up with her for so long because she was easy and gave it up to anyone who'd give us drugs."

I ground my jaw together, fisted my hands, and it was the first time I'd thought of murder. I wanted his life gone. I wanted his blood on my hands, and I would get it.

It may not be possible now, but if so, I'd relish in it.

"Wallet, PIN, card, now," he ordered, scrubbing a hand over his oily hair and then down his face, only to do it again and again.

Wallet.

My fucking wallet where I kept one of Death's alarmed pins. Standing, I said, "I'll get it."

He hummed under his breath. "Good boy."

"Do not call me boy," I snarled.

Henry chuckled, so did the other two fuckers. They moved aside and followed me into the bedroom. I listened to their comments about how sick it was that I was with a guy while I snatched up my wallet from the bedside table, opened it, and took out the pin from the back pocket. I switched it on and hit the alarm before taking out my card. Turning, I dropped the pin to the bed behind me, hoping they didn't see it while I handed over the card with my other hand.

"Here," I said, and gave him the digits to gain access. I didn't give a fuck if they took everything. I just wanted them out of the house in case any of the neighbors called the cops, and then Zion would be notified, and he'd come home. I couldn't risk him... even when I knew they wouldn't leave without hurting me. At least I knew Death would come with reinforcements.

"That the right numbers?" Henry asked, a smirk placed on his mouth, using the gun once more to scratch at his arm.

"Yes." I nodded.

He handed the gun off to one of the others and stepped closer. "Is that the right numbers?"

"Yes, why the fuck would I lie? I just want you gone." Not that they would leave, not after what I saw. Why Henry shot her in the fucking house in front of me in the first place, I didn't have a clue.... Unless he expected I wouldn't be alive to say anything to anyone.

Fuck.

Really, I'd already suspected even before he'd shot Samantha, but I'd hoped. Now hope was running out.

Henry pulled back his fist and threw it forward toward my face, but I caught it. Henry's upper lip pulled back in a snarl. He pulled his hand free. "Hold him," he ordered. The guy without the gun dragged me in front of him, pinning my arms behind my back. I struggled, but I was already sore and weakened by the hit to the head and gut. As soon as I stilled, Henry punched me in the face, the gut, and then my face again. My lip split, my eye stung like hell, and I wanted to throw up, but I breathed through it.

"Are those the right numbers?" Henry asked again.

"Yes," I ground out.

"You'd better be right." He shifted away. "I'll let you two know when to leave as soon as I get the money. You know what to do."

They didn't answer, but they must have done something because Henry walked from the room to the front door. "Have fun," he called with a chuckle before walking out and closing the door behind him.

Pain erupted in my side when one stabbed me, more pain fired through me at my face, my ribs, my leg, my gut. Over and over, they pummeled me. Some were stinging like the sharp blade slicing into my skin. I dropped to the floor and curled into myself. Still, more pain came with hits and kicks. I hated I didn't have the energy to fight back. Hated feeling exposed and vulnerable. Fucking hated it.

All while I prayed someone would come, anyone other than Zion.

"Stop, he still needs to be alive until we get the go-ahead."

Agony radiated throughout me; it was hard to stay focused, awake. All I wanted to do was close my eyes and let sleep take me away. I coughed, and blood dripped from my mouth. I didn't move to wipe it away though, not only because I didn't want to get their attention again, but I wasn't sure I could move at that point. I kept my eyes closed, feeling every throb, every ache as I stayed as still as I could.

"Did you hear that?" Thing One said.

"What?"

"Shhh." I listened to their footsteps move away from me.

Wood splintered, glass shattered, screams, and yells rose, all in seconds.

Slowly, I opened my eyes as far as I could.

"Gun, fuck. Jesus. What the fuck happened?" Death yelled.

"F-Father," I managed to get out.

"All right, kid, just stay still. Torch, we'll need paramedics for this," he called over his shoulder. I heard more curses go up and around. "Torch, soon as you've done that, go to Polished, tell Saint to get to the hospital, and you stay to take over duties."

"Why does Saint—"

"Just fuckin' do it."

"On it," he replied without further questions.

"Death" was called, and I glanced up, only to wince, and saw Quake in the doorway. "There's a dead woman out here. What we gonna do?"

"Shit, fuck. Gun—Kylo, do you know who the woman is?"

I licked my dry lips and even that hurt. "Mom."

"Fuck me, fuckin' hell, what the hell happened here? No, don't answer that. Quake, get Country on the phone. Tell him what we know so far, but let him know I'm advisin' to call this one in since Gun's goin' to the hospital."

"Got it."

"You just hang in there, Gun. We'll get this sorted."

"Z-Zion's gonna be pissed," I muttered.

"Don't you worry about him. I'll make sure he has the brothers at his back, like we'll be there for you." His hand gently ran over my head as he sat his ass down on the ground next to me.

My brothers were here.

They'd help me. They'd protect me until I could do it myself and kill the motherfucking cunt Henry.

I hummed under my breath, suddenly tired. I wanted to fade into the darkness to stop the pain radiating throughout me.

"No, Gun, not fuckin' yet. Stay with me. Stay awake."

"Can't," I breathed.

"Just a little longer, brother. I can hear the ambulance comin'. They're nearly here. Soon as they say you can, you take that nap. Just hang on a little longer."

"Hard," I mumbled.

"I know it is, Gun. Fuck, brother, please just stay awake or Saint's gonna kick my ass. You don't want that, right? Because if I have to, I'll fight back, then Saint and I'll be at ends."

"B-Bullshit," I got out, and Death chuckled.

"Yeah, you're right. It's bullshit. But I swear, if you go to sleep now, I'll kiss Saint."

I growled under my breath.

"That's right. You wouldn't want that. He's a good-lookin' motherfucker. I could totally put pussy outta my head for that guy."

"Shut it," I warned.

"They're here," I heard, followed by heavy footfalls on the porch.

Death had said I had to wait to pass out until the paramedics arrived.

They were there, so I let the darkness surround me and dove into it quickly.

CHAPTER EIGHTEEN
SAINT

Walking into the waiting area in the ER, I felt on edge, like I was going to vomit or commit murder. I first spotted Death, and when he saw me, he smiled grimly before walking toward me. He also called Quake, Country, and State with him, and I knew whatever I was about to hear wasn't good.

I stilled, my hands fisted at my sides, my jaw clenched. "Tell me?" I demanded.

"Saint, you just gotta keep your cool, brother," Country advised.

"Tell me," I snarled.

"They got into your place and hurt Gun. He's in surgery," State said.

"Who did it?" I snapped harshly.

Country moved closer, and his hand landed on my shoulder. "Breathe and fuckin' listen," he ordered. He didn't go on until I took a breath. Only it didn't settle me; instead, it had me burning hotter for fucking revenge. Country shook his head. "All right, you're gonna lose it, but you can't do it here, or you won't get in to see him. Keep a fuckin' lid on it until you're outside."

I nodded. I needed more than anything to see Kylo.

"Right, from what we'd gathered, Gun's parents showed. The

father, Henry, shot the mother, Samantha, and killed her in the house. Two others were there. They've been taken by the police. Henry wasn't there when we got there, but the brothers got out of one of the fuckers before the cops arrived that Henry had taken off with Gun's bank card and PIN."

"Find him," I said roughly.

Country nodded. "We will. I have everyone out there lookin'."

I closed my eyes and sucked in a breath. "How bad…?"

A breath later, I opened my eyes, watching as Death moved in when Country stepped back. His hand cupped the back of my neck. "Broken ribs, stab wounds, beaten black and blue. It ain't gonna be good to see, but your man will need you."

Christ. Fucking Christ.

My whole body broke out in shivers, my gut twisting painfully, and I wanted to drop to my knees at the agony clenching my heart.

"Fuck," I uttered.

The door behind us opened, and I heard boomed, "Where the fuck is our son?"

Turning, I saw Boom enter, his arm around a crying Wendy. They headed straight for me. I straightened and ground my teeth together. When they stopped, and before they could say anything, I spoke. "It's my fault. I wasn't there to help him, and he got hurt. I understand—"

"Enough," Boom said loudly. He clasped my arm in a grip and shook it. "No one expected this to happen. It ain't your fuckin' fault, Saint. You above anythin' make him happy."

"He's right," Wendy said with a sniffle and a small, sad smile.

Boom dropped his hold and looked to Country. "I want time with the people who did this."

"The two that were there are in custody, Boom," State explained.

Boom shook his head. "Know that. Death explained what went down. I mean the motherfuckin' cunt of a so-called sperm donor who brought our kid into the world. Can't believe I was fuckin' friends with that motherfuckin' cunt." He ended on a yell, grabbing attention from more people in the waiting room.

"Boom, you wanna keep it down before you get kicked out and don't get to see your son?"

"Fuck." He sighed. "I'm takin' Wendy to get a coffee. Call me if you hear anythin', and I mean anythin'."

Since he was looking at me when he spoke, I nodded. He gave me a chin lift while Wendy smiled softly with tears in her eyes, and they both turned toward the elevators. People got out of his way quickly. He was a big man, loud, but had a huge heart.

I moved over to a row of seats and sat, bending to rest my elbows on my knees and put my head in my hands. Closing my eyes, I breathed out slowly. Waiting wasn't my strong suit, but I'd wait for-fucking-ever for Kylo.

He had to be okay. He had to pull through, and we'd hunt the cunt down together to get revenge. He would die for what he did. Die by our own hands. But not before he paid in as much pain as we could deliver.

A weight sat in my chest. A dead, sad weight, and it wouldn't go away until I was at Kylo's side. Until I knew he would be okay. I didn't care about the weight. I wanted it. I'd hold it and let it grow until he opened his eyes.

"Right, I should probably mention—" Death started.

"What's going on?" I heard asked loudly and stood to see Lucas and Wreck just inside the doors.

"That I called Lucas and Wreck as well, since they're friends," Death finished.

Lucas spotted me and made his way over. He stopped in front of me, opened his mouth, and snapped it closed when he took me in. His brows dipped. "Why do you look upset? Is he okay? Is Kylo okay?"

Death answered, "We don't know yet. They're operatin'. When he got sliced, they nicked somethin' important."

Lucas paled, then nodded. Wreck stepped up behind him,

placing his hands on Lucas's hips for support. "He'll be okay. He will be."

"He's strong," Wreck added.

Lucas nodded again. "He is." He pulled his gaze back up to me. "But… it doesn't explain why you look devastated."

"I…." I snapped my mouth closed and clenched my jaw. It wasn't the right time for Lucas to know since Kylo was hurt, but I wasn't going to hide my anguish.

Lucas crossed his arms over his chest. "You hardly know him. Why do you care so much?"

"Because he's mine."

Wreck's eyes flashed, but they settled, unlike Lucas's—even his mouth dropped open. He took a deep breath, and I knew I was going to get a talking to before he even started with, "What do you mean he's yours? You can't mean like I think you mean because that's just stupid. You've never once looked at a guy before, and what, you now think you can fool around with Kylo and his feelings? I won't let it happen. You do not get to mess with him like that." He glared, his chest heaved with every breath, and his fist was in my face. "Ouch, dammit," he complained after hitting me.

I rubbed at my cheek, looking at him. "What was that for?" I demanded.

Lucas ignored me and started shaking his hand out. "You broke my hand with your dang hard face. Wade, Wade, he broke my hand. He broke my wacking hand." Wreck's lips twitched, but he brought Lucas into his arms and gently checked his hand over.

"It's bruised, but not broken," Wreck assured him.

"Stupid boofhead." He glared at me.

"I could have gone without knowin' which hand you jerk off with," Death put in.

Lucas stilled, blinked, no doubt realizing he'd overshared. He groaned, turning to me with another glare like it was my fault he'd blurted it.

"Why did you hit me?" I asked.

"Because… well, you hit Wade when you thought he was just messing with me. I don't want you to play with Kylo. He—"

"I'm not, and I won't. What Kylo and I have is serious, and it'll continue no matter what happens."

"You've never been with a guy before, you—"

"Neither had Wreck, but you were all okay about that. Can't you just believe I'm in it for the good reasons? I want Kylo in my life." I threw my hands up in frustration. "I know I've never even thought about bein' with a guy before. Maybe my eyes hadn't been opened to the possibility until the right guy came along. Yeah, I've known Kylo for a long time, but it wasn't until we spent some time together did I understand I wanted more from him."

Lucas studied me, then sighed. "I can't argue with that." He glanced back at Wreck before facing me again. "But if you hurt him, I will harm you. Just remember, I know the body a lot more than anyone."

I nodded. "Got it, bro. But I'd never hurt him, not intentionally."

"Fine, I'm going to get ice for my hand."

He didn't believe me completely, and I couldn't blame him. I'd been the same when I found out about him and Wreck. Eventually, he'd see how serious I was about Kylo. Until then, I wasn't going to waste my time or breath convincing him. Instead, I sat back down. Death sat beside me, but I didn't pay attention to him or anyone around me. I buried my head in my hands again, closed my eyes, and prayed that everything would be all right with Kylo.

"FAMILY FOR KYLO—"

"Here," Boom yelled.

I stood, my heart beating so hard it near made me dizzy. Boom curled an arm around Wendy as they moved closer to the doctor. I stepped up with them, along with the others waiting for news. My gut churned, my ears waiting, and my eyes clung to the doctor in case he disappeared and I'd dreamed his arrival.

"Good news, he's out of surgery, awake, but tired and dazed. Would you like to see him?"

Relief flooded my system. Suddenly it was easier to breathe.

It surprised me when they looked my way. I shook my head. "You guys go first."

Wendy smiled softly. She reached out, and I took her hand as it squeezed around mine. "We won't be long."

I nodded. "It's okay, take your time."

After another squeeze, they walked through the doors.

Fuck. Thank you, Lord. Thank you.

I smiled down at my feet as a hand gently grasped the back of my neck. "He's good," Death said.

Smiling at him, I replied, "Yeah, he is, and we'll get the fucker who did this, so he'll be even better."

"Damn right. Breathe easy, brother."

"So," Lucas drew out, stepping up beside me, "who knows about you and Kylo?"

Death snorted, and he moved off, probably not wanting to join in on the conversation.

"I gathered Boom and Wendy know. Death obviously does as well."

"Country, State, a few other brothers since now, plus... Mom and Dad."

His eyes widened. "Are you serious?"

"Yeah, he was there the day after I got shot. Dad shoved him in the pantry."

His mouth dropped open, and I heard a deep chuckle from behind, knowing it was Wreck.

"They didn't say anything. I'm surprised Mom acted so well."

"So was I."

I swung my gaze to the doors when they opened. Boom and Wendy walked back out, both smiling.

"I said to take your time," I told them, shaking my head.

Wendy rested her hand on my arm. "It's okay. We just needed to see he was good. He's sleepy and wants to see you."

Elation swelled inside me. More than anything, I wanted to see him before he slept.

"Lucas?"

"No. You go."

"No, bro, he'll be happy to see you, and I know you won't settle like us until you do see him."

"Are you sure?"

"Yeah." I hooked my arm around Lucas, got the details of Kylo's room, then headed beyond the doors.

"We'll get him through this," Lucas said softly.

"We will," I agreed. Dropping my arm from my brother, I opened Kylo's door and stepped in. Only to still. I wasn't sure why I didn't expect all the bruising, but I didn't, and for a beat, it took me by surprise. My gut twisted as if someone stabbed me right there.

"Fuck," I uttered.

Kylo was already looking at me. "I'm okay," he whispered.

"Fuck," I uttered again. Fisting my hands, I went to the side of the bed and started to reach for him but pulled back. I didn't know where I could touch him without hurting him. I didn't want to hurt him more than he already was.

He reached out, and that drew me out of my own thoughts. I took his hand and leaned toward him to gently rest my forehead against his.

"Baby," I whimpered, my eyes welling with tears.

"I'm okay," he said again. When I groaned, he added, "I will be at least."

Shifting back, I ran my fingers through his hair. "You will. I'll make sure of it. I'm sorry—"

"Don't. They set it all up—" He yawned, then winced.

"Sleep, lover."

"Will you stay?" he asked.

I gave him a smile. "No one could get rid of me." Kissing his temple, I reached back and pulled a chair close. Still holding his hand, I sat and glided my fingers up and down his arm softly. It only took seconds before his eyes fluttered closed.

A sniffle caught my attention. I swung my gaze to the doorway.

Hell, I'd forgot Lucas had come in with me.

He wiped at his eyes with the back of his hands. "I see it now." He nodded and smiled. "I mean, I wish I knew from the start, but I can't say anything because Wade and I did the same thing. I'm happy for you both."

"Thanks, Lucas." I looked back to Kylo. "I'm happy too."

It was then I knew, as if everything clicked into place inside me, I wouldn't give Kylo up. He was in my heart, my mind, and my soul. He was mine, and I wanted my future with him in it. I didn't care how it worked out, but I'd be calling him mine. My lover, my one and only, my damn husband.

Maybe it was too soon for that deep shit, but I'd start out small.

After I found a new house, one Kylo wasn't hurt in and wouldn't see his dead mother on the floor, then I'd move Kylo in with me.

I'd get to fall asleep and wake up beside him. We'd cook, eat, watch TV together like we already did, but it'd be more because we'd be doing it knowing we loved each other.

Glancing to Lucas, I asked, "Do you think I could get the name of the real estate lady you guys used?"

"Of course, though… she's a bit of a flirt."

"Someone else then," I said, nodding to myself.

"I'll find someone for you."

"Thanks, bro."

"I'm guessing you're staying in here?"

I laughed. "Yeah, until they kick me out. That's if I let them."

"I'll be out with Wade and the rest."

"Go get some rest," I told him.

He shook his head. "No. I… we're all a family. We all stand by each other. We'll wait."

"Lucas, I know what you mean, I do. But he'll be sleeping for the rest of the night. Please, so I know everyone else is good, get everyone out there to go home and sleep. Kylo will want to see them tomorrow, and I mean you as well."

He took a moment and finally nodded. "Okay."

"Thank you."

"Get some rest too."

I nodded. "Soon." After Lucas left, I couldn't keep my eyes off Kylo. It hurt my fucking heart seeing the state he was in, but he would heal physically, and I'd help him emotionally. If I couldn't, I would get someone who could.

Dipping, I kissed his hand in mine and rested my forehead against it. "Never scare me like this again, baby. I can't take it. Love you too damn much."

CHAPTER NINETEEN
KYLO

*S*oft lips woke me when they kissed their way from my neck up to my mouth. Reaching up, I wound my arms around Zion's neck and held him close. I felt him smile against my mouth.

"Mornin'," he greeted, pulling back from me.

Opening my eyes, the rest of sleep evaporated, and my mind wasn't the only thing that woke. My dick gave a throb under the blankets at seeing Zion resting over me with an arm at each side of my head. "Mornin' to you too."

"Gotta go, lover, but your breakfast is beside the bed."

My stomach fluttered. "You do know I can get my own." It'd been a month since I got out of the hospital. I was almost healed, but it was my leg that still ached whenever I walked, well limped, around with a cane. I was told it might heal completely over time, or there was a possibility I would always walk with a limp. At first, the idea scared me, but Zion reminded me that I was alive and that was all that mattered.

He'd been right.

"Know that, but I wanted to."

He wanted to do a lot of things for me. He'd slept at my side since coming home to Boom and Wendy's. He'd held me close every night, didn't push for anything sexual. He was just there, wanted to be here for me, and I couldn't be giddier over it than I already was.

He was perfect.

He also didn't want me at his house since that was where my attack happened, even when I kept telling him I was fine staying at his place. To me, it didn't matter it was where Samantha died or where I'd been beaten. It was Zion's home, was where he lived, and that was all that mattered. Yet, he refused, saying he was doing some redecorating and wanted me at Boom's where I would be safe and warm. It helped that he stayed with me every night, or I would have fought harder to go where he was, where he lived.

I was falling hard for Zion Storey. So much so, I was fucking in love with him.

"Then thank you," I told him, brushing a stray piece of hair from his eyes.

"Anythin'," he said, his voice thicker than usual. He dipped and went to kiss me again, but I covered my mouth quickly.

"Morning breath," I mumbled behind my hand.

He chuckled and pulled my hand away. "I don't care." He dipped again and pressed his mouth against mine. My stomach fluttered again, my cock throbbing, and I wrapped my arms around his shoulders when he deepened the kiss. I loved waking with him. I loved how he kissed me, how he cared for me, how he did sweet things like making me breakfast when he didn't have to but wanted to.

I just loved him.

He broke the kiss with a final peck of my lips. "I have to go," he said, but he didn't make a move to leave.

I ran my hand over his stubble, one that I liked feeling whenever we did kiss since that was all we'd done in a long time. In fact, I was tired of not having him in ways I wanted him. He'd evaded every teasing touch I'd given when I tried to reach past his waistband with a chuckle and one word of "Soon."

Soon had better be tonight because I was ready to feel all of him inside me.

Fuck me, I sounded like a horndog, but I couldn't help it. I was so damn horny.

"Are you goin'?"

He grinned. "Yes."

"It doesn't look like it," I teased.

"I will. You have West and Lucas dropping by today."

"I know. I do remember things."

His brows rose, and I flicked his nose. "I do, asshole."

He snorted. "All right then." With another quick peck, he straightened and walked toward the door. "Behave yourself."

"I always do."

"Not when you're around West and Lucas."

I laughed. "We're talkin' about the same West and Lucas, right?"

He turned and nodded. "We are. I've known Lucas all my life. The little shit was always up to somethin'. He might be quiet and shy, but he's a mastermind underneath all that. West… I'm not too sure about. But if he's friends with my brother, I need to be wary."

Rolling my eyes, I flicked my hand his way, then slowly sat up. "We'll be fine. Hell, I feel like a stay-at-home kept woman with her friends coming over for coffee while my man goes off to work."

Chuckling to myself, I rested back against the headboard and glanced over to Zion when he hadn't said anything. His eyes darkened, and he clipped, "Say it again."

My brows dipped when confusion swept over me. "What?"

"That I'm your man."

My heart skipped a beat and sped off with my pulse. "You're my man."

He stalked back over to the bed. I leaned forward eagerly, waiting for his mouth, only he grabbed the back of my hair and tilted my head back in a hard grip. "I am yours. It means you're mine as well."

I gave him a teasing smile. "I thought we'd known this since I can't seem to get rid of you."

He shook his head, a smirk playing at his lips. "You'd never want to get rid of me."

He was right. I wouldn't.

With a wink, he leaned in, kissed my neck, and walked toward the door again. "See you later," he called.

"Later." I shot him a chin lift before he moved out and shut the door behind him. I probably had about half an hour to eat, shower, and get dressed before Wendy came in and fussed over me. I didn't have it in me to tell her I didn't need her assistance. She liked helping, and eventually, I wouldn't be living under their roof where she could give it so freely. Plus, I did enjoy having a mother who cared enough to dote on me.

Still, the one thing I refused was help in the bathroom. I had to get my ass out of bed and get organized for the day.

"No one has heard anything?" West asked. Just after Lucas and West arrived, I took them into the dining room to sit around the kitchen table, since Wendy had cooked us some lunch.

I honestly did feel like a kept woman with friends over to gossip.

I shook my head. "Not a word. The cops haven't gotten any information on his whereabouts either." I wouldn't lose hope though. One day Henry would slip up and we'd find the fucker. It would then be my chance to deal out the punishment he deserved. At first, I'd been reserved about telling the cops anything, but when Zion explained they had to be called in since Henry shot Samantha in the house, an ambulance had been called, and the other two motherfuckers who'd assisted Henry got taken into custody, I didn't have much of a choice but to tell them everything. I'd been surprised they didn't judge me for who I was and try and pin something on me. Shit like that had happened before to the brothers in the club. However, there was enough evidence to back everything up, but I also had to think the cops *I* had to deal with were some of the few good ones.

"Where could he have gone?" Lucas thought aloud.

I shrugged. "Anyway, I don't want to think about that fucker. How are you two doin'? Only a couple of months before you guys graduate and go into med school. Lookin' forward to it?"

"If I pass," West grumbled.

Lucas slapped his arm. "You will."

"Will the change in jobs help with study time or anythin'?" I asked. We'd both heard from Death just the other day saying he had a couple of openings coming up, and if we wanted the jobs, they were ours. Zion was happy for me, and I really didn't want to go back to Polished. I didn't want to go on pretend dates when I had Zion. I snapped up the job, and West told me he did the same. However, he was still working at Polished until he could start the new one.

"Maybe, I'll have to see, but staying at Lucas's has helped with the money situation."

Lucas reached out and slapped West's arm again. "I still can't believe you didn't tell me you're on a scholarship and your parents weren't helping you out with anything."

Somehow, when I'd still been in the hospital, and they'd come to visit, West opened up to both of us about things he hadn't shared before. His parents were religious. As such, they didn't know West was gay because they saw it was wrong in God's eyes. They refused to help West with living away from home because they had wanted him to stay with them while in college, but West felt he couldn't be himself.

I didn't blame him. It would have been suffocating living with parents like that.

West rolled his eyes. "It's not something I wanted people to know, but..." He glanced away toward the kitchen, where Wendy puttered around over our lunch. Yeah, I was spoilt. He looked back to us, and I caught the color rising in his cheeks. "I haven't been close to anyone like I have you two." He played with his drink, moving the glass around so the Coke would swish around the edges. "Not in school, not out of it, until meeting Lucas and then you, Kylo, through him."

Lucas lunged and wrapped his arms around West, who rocked sideways on his seat. He grabbed the edge of the table to steady them both. West caught my gaze and rolled his eyes again. He was also softly smiling like I was.

Lucas pulled back, his face on fire, burning brighter than West's was. "You both know I didn't have any friends before you two either." He pointed at me. "And I know you had your brothers in the club, but we're different, and you can't say you don't love us."

"You're right."

Lucas jerked his head back, shocked. "I am?"

Chuckling, I nodded. "Yeah, not to get all mushy, but I'm closer to you guys than anyone. Well, except Zion."

Lucas snorted. "Another thing I still can't believe, you taming my brother, the man whore."

"I got skills," I said with a grin.

"And I don't need to know about those skills," Lucas said.

"He's very smitten," West commented. "Actually, you all are, and it kind of makes me ill."

I raised a brow. "Heard anythin' from your mystery guy?"

West had also told Lucas why he needed to leave Polished, besides the problem of it getting out when he was a full-fledged doctor.

West shook his head. "Nope."

"He'll come around," Lucas said.

West laughed, but there wasn't any trace of humor in it. "I was just company for him. I don't need the hassle of a relationship at the moment anyway. Not with final exams coming up. Besides, he wasn't in it for a relationship. Like I'd told Kylo, I wasn't even sure he was gay or bi."

"He'd have to be or else he wouldn't have set anything up in the first place," Lucas said.

"I agree," I added in.

West shook his head. "It doesn't matter anyway." When Wendy walked into the dining room, I heard West mutter, "Good timing."

"Lunchtime," Wendy sang.

"Thanks, Wendy," I said, smiling up at her as she set a tray of burritos down on the table.

She straightened and rested her hand on my shoulder. "You're welcome, honey. Do you guys need anything else? Another drink?"

"I think we're good. Why don't you join us for lunch?" I asked.

"I'd love to, but Lucy is calling shortly. We're going to go over some recipes." She ruffled my hair and went back into the kitchen. Lucy, Lucas and Zion's mom, and Wendy had met in the hospital when they'd both been to visit and bonded over, well, being mothers, I guessed. They became fast friends, much as I had with Lucas and West. It was good to see as Wendy had a few brothers' old ladies as friends, but she could always do with more, and Lucy was just as kickass as Wendy was.

"They'll be on the phone for hours," Lucas said.

I snorted. "I heard Boom the other day askin' Wendy if she loved Lucy more than him. Let's just say it was a little tense for a moment when she didn't answer." They both chuckled.

"I think it's great they're getting along so well," Lucas said.

"It's good to see," I agreed. Something else that was good was how all the brothers had accepted Zion and me as a… well, couple. Zion said he'd gotten a few questions, ones like whose pussy was it that got him to switch teams—so they knew to steer clear—and some strange looks, but other than that, no one had said anything bad. What helped was Wreck getting in with Lucas and Lucas being Zion's brother.

Even if they hadn't taken it well, it didn't matter.

Zion made me happy.

Fucking ecstatic.

Yeah, it still surprised me when I really thought about it—that Zion was mine. Yet, with every day that passed, it felt normal. Like we were supposed to happen.

I still had a feeling, even though Zion denied it, that it was my blow job skills that had him stalking after me.

"We've lost him," West commented.

"What?" I asked, pushing my plate away, seeing they'd been eating their own burritos while my mind drifted.

They both laughed. Lucas shook his head and asked West, "I wasn't that bad, right?"

West snorted. "You're still that bad."

"What the fuck you two talkin' about?" I barked.

"Getting that lost, soft look on your face when you think of Zion," Lucas said.

"Not that I do, but West is right. You still get a dopey look on your face when you think of Wreck."

"I never said dopey," West put in.

Lucas glared. "Shut up. I do not."

West sighed. "Both of you get stupid over your other, *cough*, better half. It's cute. Don't stress over it."

"Fuck off, I'm not like that," I said, just as my cell rang. I pulled it close and saw Zion's name on the screen. I couldn't stop the smile from forming.

"See, that right there." Lucas pointed.

I gave him the finger and then answered the call, "Miss me already?"

"Always," he replied straightaway. "I have news."

I stilled. Both Lucas and West straightened when they noticed. "What?"

"We've got him."

"Are you serious?"

"Yep. Boom brought him in. We got him in one of the cells below." The compound had a secret basement below where we kept our armory when we needed to deal with anyone who wanted to fuck with the club. It also contained three cells where we dealt out punishments. Zion went on, "I'm on my way to grab you."

"I'll be ready." As soon as Zion hung up, I looked to Lucas and West.

From overhearing the conversation, Lucas and West gave me a nod. They knew what I wanted when it came to Henry. They weren't a fan of my choice but still respected it since it was the way of the brotherhood when it came to our payback.

"We'll talk soon," West said as he stood.

"Be careful," Lucas added.

"I will." I nodded. I walked them to the door and said goodbye, but not before Lucas gave me a quick hug. Then I went into the bedroom to change into clothes I wouldn't mind getting dirty.

CHAPTER TWENTY
SAINT

It was understandable the drive to the compound was quiet. When we pulled in and got out, I met Kylo at the front of the car and tugged him to a stop with my hand in his.

"What do you want to happen in there?" I asked. I didn't want to bring it up on the drive since it looked like Kylo needed his silence to process we had his father in lockup and was about to deliver some payback.

"I want him in pain. I want him to suffer, and I want both of us to deliver it."

Nodding, I took his hand in mine, pulled it up, and kissed it. "Then we'll make it happen."

He tugged me into him, dropped my hand, and wound his arm around my waist. "Thank you for being you, for takin' a chance on us, and for standin' at my side."

My chest compressed, then expanded. "Anythin' for you."

We both leaned in. Our lips pressed, opened, and tasted.

"It's sweet and all, but let's get this show on the road." We broke apart to see Death approaching us.

"Don't get jealous on me, Death. We'll make out later," I teased with a wink.

Death grinned. Kylo growled under his breath. "Like hell," he clipped, causing Death and me to chuckle.

We made our way into the compound when Death said, "Don't worry, Gun, he's all yours. Blonds just don't do it for me."

Kylo grunted. "Good."

We stopped in the common room where other brothers were. They took us in, giving us a greeting in some way. Country, State, and Wreck approached us, but it was Country who said, "You gotta make a decision, Gun. In the end, do we turn him over or make sure the cops never find him?"

"He's never to be found again," Kylo stated.

It was what I would have picked. No one fucked with us. *No one* fucked with the Diamond MC, but more importantly, no one fucked with my man.

Squeezing his hand, I smiled and nodded my approval as Kylo met my gaze.

They parted, and we walked through, heading toward the basement area. I wasn't sure what Kylo was feeling. I wished I could read his mind in case he needed something from me. But I wanted to end this so Kylo could breathe easy and move on with his life. There might be other hurdles, other challenges in life, but we'd deal with them together. We'd have the brothers at our backs, but we'd also have each other.

There wasn't anything that would keep me away from Kylo.

Nothing.

I didn't know if Kylo understood how deep I'd fallen, but I had.

Walking down the stairs, I stopped at the bottom when Kylo moved up to my side. Boom waited, leaning against the wall.

"Boom" was all Kylo said.

"Kid," Boom replied. "I held back. Wasn't sure what you'd pick."

"Saint and I will go in there and finish this."

Boom straightened as he looked at Kylo with pride and nodded once. He made it our way, dropped a hand to Kylo's shoulder, and I caught the pressure he applied before he moved up the stairs.

"Let us know if you need anythin'," Country said at our back.

State nodded in agreement. "We'll wait around in case." Wreck grunted, his way of saying he'd be there too.

"Thanks, brothers," Kylo said before he went down the hall to where the cell was. Where his father waited. I followed silently behind him. He didn't hesitate when we got to the cell. He took the key off the hook and unlocked the door. With a final touch from me, my hand to his back, he flung the door wide.

Henry sat on a cot in the corner. He stood when we'd entered, winced, holding his ribs on his right side. Yeah, Boom had his fun.

He started rambling, "Kylo, son, I didn't mean anything by it. I wasn't myself." He hit the side of his head with his hand. "I-I'm messed up." Tears sprung to his bruised eyes. "I'll get help. I will. I won't let it happen again. I promise. If you just let me go, I won't do drugs, drink, nothing. Please, just let me go. I'll get your money back. I will. I'll disappear. You won't see me again. I won't come near you." He flicked his gaze to me. "To any of you."

"You killed her," Kylo said, his voice like steel.

Henry cringed. Tears fell as he whispered, "I wasn't myself."

"You murdered your wife," Kylo snarled, his upper lip pulling up in disgust.

"I didn't mean it," Henry sobbed.

"You came into Saint's house, killed Samantha, beat me, and you thought you would have the chance for me to leave you alone?"

"Kylo, please, please, I didn't mean anything. I was high, out of my head." He slapped the sides of his head again. "I just needed money. I needed money."

Kylo snorted. "You're pathetic."

He dropped to his knees, his hands out. "Please, *please*, Kylo, let me go. Don't call the cops. Don't send me to jail. Please. I won't be able to take it. Please, please, Kylo."

"Get up," Kylo demanded.

Henry didn't move.

"You heard him. Get the fuck up," I barked.

Henry whimpered.

Fuck me.

Fucking hell, he *was* pathetic.

Kylo snorted. "I never said anythin' about jail or the cops, Henry. You ain't that lucky."

Henry's eyes widened, more panic setting in.

Good.

He deserved everything we would deal out.

"No," Henry whispered. "You wouldn't do that to me."

I shook my head and smiled while Kylo laughed darkly. "What? Kill you like you did Samantha? Like you and those other fuckers would have done to me?"

He winced and swallowed thickly. His eyes flicked behind us toward the door. Slowly, he stood, and I knew, I fucking knew he was going to try and make a break for it.

He shifted from one foot to the other, and then it was like something inside of him had been switched on. He scowled at Kylo and snarled, "You can't do this. You won't want to go to jail for killing me." He laughed. "Then again, you'd probably like it, right? Like a good fucking up the ass. Bet your boy here does you good, you fucking disgusting piece of shit."

Kylo raised a brow and asked, "You done?"

He spat to the side before calling Kylo every name under the sun. I listened, watching closely. The stupid cunt edged toward the door. We moved with him, letting him think we were so distracted by his words that he could just escape.

I wanted to laugh at him. Laugh in his face and then kick it.

Henry lunged for the door. Kylo dropped his cane, spun around, hooked an arm around his neck, and threw Henry across the room. He landed with a bang and moaned.

I stared at Kylo because that was fucking hot.

Kylo moved toward him with a limp. I hung back and let Kylo have his way until he needed me. With a strength I knew was fueled by his rage, Kylo picked Henry up by his tee and punched him in the face.

"That was for Samantha."

He hit him again in the face before Henry could recover and snarled, "That was for me."

Kylo dropped him. Immediately, Henry moaned and started begging again. With a fluid motion, Kylo pulled a knife out of the back of his jeans and unsheathed it. He threw the cover down, hauled Henry up, and pushed him up against the wall.

"You fuckin' think you get to live in this world when you've done damn nothin' but tarnish it?" He stabbed the knife into Henry's side. Henry groaned and cried out. "You're worthless. You're nothin'. The best fuckin' thing you did for me was give me over to Boom. Other than that, you're a waste of space, and the world will be better without you." He withdrew the knife and planted it in Henry's thigh.

Henry's screams were like music to my ears.

"Saint," Kylo called.

"Yeah, babe?"

"Come have your fun before I end this fucker's life. I don't want to waste any more time on him."

"You're right. He ain't worth it," I said as I walked over. "Drop him," I added.

Kylo did, and Henry fell to the floor, whimpering and moaning in pain.

Good.

Pulling back my foot, I kicked the motherfucker in the gut, the face, the legs. I wanted every inch of him in pain. Every fucking inch.

Panting, I crouched in front of him and gripped his oily hair in my fist, tugging up his head so he could look at me through his swollen eyes. "You know you're gonna die." His eyes flared to what they could. Fear rolled off him. He reeked of it. "You shouldn't have come after him. You shouldn't have laid a hand on him, or had those fuckers, who will pay in jail, touch him. Kylo's ours. He's Diamond, but more importantly, he's mine." I wound a hand around his neck and shifted him up the wall, so he sat on the floor. My grip tightened, cutting off his oxygen. He tried to fight, tried to pry my hand away, but I held on and watched him struggle until he near passed out.

Letting go, I stood and shifted back.

Kylo lifted his chin toward me and moved in.

Henry shifted his gaze, seeing Kylo tap the knife against his thigh while he looked in disgust down at the man who helped bring him into the world.

Kylo didn't say anything as he slowly leaned down and forward, the knife held out in front of him. Henry went to grab it, but I got there and knocked his working hand away. A second later, Kylo dug the tip of the knife into Henry's skin at his neck.

"Enjoy your time in hell, motherfucker," he bit out and sliced the knife across Henry's throat. It cut in deeply, blood squirting and coating the front of Henry, Kylo's arms, and the floor.

When Kylo stood and stepped back, I moved close to his side, and we stayed there until the life drifted from Henry's eyes and he slumped back against the wall.

"He deserved it," I said.

Kylo nodded. "He did."

I ran my fingers over his hand. "You okay?"

Kylo shrugged, glancing at me. "Maybe I should feel bad for takin' a life, but I don't."

"I was the same when I took my first," I said.

"When?" he asked.

"Just after I got patched in. You remember the attack we had here at the compound?"

"Yeah, I heard Boom talkin' about the fuckers who wanted to take on Diamond so they could deal cocaine in our area."

I nodded. "I killed to protect the club, to protect the brothers, and I don't regret it."

"Club is life," Kylo said.

"It is." I took his hand as he threw the knife to the ground beside

Henry's lifeless body. "Come on, let's go get cleaned up. We'll grab some drinks after in the common room. Surround ourselves with the brothers."

"Sounds fuckin' good."

WE KNEW the brothers would clean up our mess, so I took Kylo to my room in the compound. Only when I opened the door, I realized my mistake when I saw the brochures on my bed.

"What's that?" he asked when I stilled.

Shifting over to the bed, I collected them, but Kylo was right there next to me. He picked one up. "You lookin' at buyin' a place?" he groaned. "Zion, please tell me it's not because of what happened at your house with me?"

"It's not," I said quickly.

"Zion—"

"Been wantin' to move for a while. The 'rents have never liked the area I'm in, and I'm over worryin' about gettin' my shit stolen." I shrugged and took the brochure from his hands. "It's time to move."

He sighed, leaned his cane next to the bed, and took my hand in his to tug me into him. I met his gaze when he said, "You liked that place. I don't know if I've ever said sorry it happened—"

"Don't you fuckin' dare. I hate that it happened, but I don't care it was at my place. I want to move, Kylo. I need this. A new chapter in life, and I want you to move in with me."

He bit his bottom lip and studied me for a beat before shaking his head, and my gut clenched. "No."

"No?"

"Nope, it's too soon, but it doesn't change how I feel about you. Hell, I might even end up stayin' at your place most of the time, but I ain't movin' in."

"Yet, right?"

He rolled his eyes. "Maybe."

I pouted.

He snorted. "Don't fuckin' pout at me."

"But, lover, I need my boo boo in my house all the damn time to perv on."

He laughed, and it was good to see some of his light shining back in there. Taking a life took a toll on you; I knew it, felt it, but with the support at our backs, Kylo would be fine. Especially since we knew what a piece of shit Henry had been.

I'd keep an eye on him in case it did play with his mind. If we couldn't help, then I'd find someone we could trust who he could share this shit with.

Yeah, I'd keep a close eye on him.

He was mine to take care of, to protect over anyone.

I knew he was holding back moving in with me because he was still worried about this lasting. I'd give him time, and eventually, he'd see I wouldn't go anywhere except for where he was.

"Not happenin', but would sharin' a shower help your delicate feelin's?"

"Hmm, it could, for a start."

"Then that's what we'll do. I'll get you drunk later and suck you off."

"Now we're talkin', but we'll be bringin' the matter of movin' in with me up at a later date… like tomorrow."

He chuckled and led me toward the bathroom off my bedroom. "We'll see."

I'd wear him down with my flowery words and sweep him off his feet to a point he couldn't say no anymore. Well, eventually I would.

CHAPTER TWENTY-ONE
KYLO

"At least it's only another couple of months, and you'll get out of Polished and into security," I said to West on the phone as I sat in bed waiting on Zion to get home. I hadn't let Zion know Wendy and Boom wouldn't be here, which I planned to use to my advantage. Lucas and Wreck had visited Zion's house earlier. They had happened to go there, though, when Zion wasn't home so they could find something for me.

I glanced to the side and grinned at the guitar.

Lucas already knew Zion played the guitar since he was his brother, but he hadn't known he'd kept it going into his adult life. He'd thought Zion had stopped in high school. Wreck didn't give a shit whether Zion played or not. He didn't care about much unless it had something to do with Lucas. So at least I knew they wouldn't blab to the brothers until Zion was ready to show his skills.

Skills I was keen on seeing tonight.

West sighed through the phone. "I know. At least then you'll be working there as well."

"Exactly." It worried me I hadn't worked since being injured, but Zion, Country, and Death had all stated I had to heal to a point I was able to move without so much pain before I started back in on any job. It just happened to be about the same time I would be starting at the security firm. What eased my concerns and stopped me arguing with them about work was that the bank replaced all the money Henry stole, which had only been finalized last week. It helped me breathe a bit easier knowing I had money to back me up from not working for so long.

Zion had tried to tell me he'd support me when it came to money, but I didn't want to rely on someone else. It took him a while to understand. He saw it as since we were together, whatever he had in life was mine as well. I found the whole thing mind-blowing, and I figured I was still getting used to the idea Zion was mine. Eventually, he'd understood that I wasn't throwing away his offer, that I would take him up on it if necessary. Though I was sure he just said so to appease me. The truth was I needed to manage without laying my shit on someone else. I needed to be independent.

"You are okay with leavin' Polished, right?" I asked since West was quiet.

"Yes, yeah, I am…."

"But?" I pressed.

"Yesterday I was talking with Lucas and realized I missed him."

"The client?" I asked to clarify.

He laughed humorlessly. "It's stupid. We hardly spoke, but I liked being around him. Why can't I get over this?"

I didn't want to voice the answer I had, which was that he could have been the one for West, like Zion was for me, but saying that could hurt him more. I didn't know this guy, but they'd connected on a different level than West had with his ex, and West had thought he'd loved Sam.

"You will eventually. It just takes time."

"It's been nearly two months, Kylo," he stated.

I cringed. "Fuck, I know. Sorry. Why don't you come over here and we'll chat while we get drunk?"

He laughed a little. "Thanks for the offer, but it's late. I'm about to head home, and Saint just left to get to you. I'm not interrupting that. Still—"

"West? Somethin' wrong?"

"Huh? Oh, no, I just thought I saw someone I knew. Thanks for the chat, but I'll talk to you soon."

"You got it. Take care."

"Thanks, you too." He hung up, and I placed my phone on the bedside table. I worried about West and figured a guys' night was called for with West, Lucas, and me. And soon.

For now, I wanted to make sure everything was ready for when Zion got home. I'd already showered, so I got undressed, put his guitar at the end of the bed, and sat naked on the bed with a book beside me and my comics.

It was time to trade.

Since Boom had given Zion a key after saying, "Looks like you're stickin' around, so here, Gun wants you to have a key and thought it's better comin' from me since it's my place and all," I'd have to listen out for the key in the door.

However, while I waited, I picked up the current paperback, which I quickly got lost in, so when a throat cleared from the doorway, I jumped.

"So, you read naked?" Zion teased with a smirk.

I chuckled, my face heating. "Not usually. Only when I know my man is comin' home."

He stepped into the room and closed our door. "I'm guessin' Boom and Wendy won't be home."

"You guessed right," I told him.

He paused, removing his vest when he spotted his guitar. His eyes lifted to me, his brow shooting up.

"I didn't go there," I said. Zion still wouldn't let me there until he moved into his new place. "Lucas was happy to grab it for me."

He snorted. "Of course he was." He placed his vest over the chaise lounge and removed his tee, dropping it to the floor. "Let me guess if I have this situation straight. You want me to play you a song, and I'll get to listen to a book?" His gaze shifted to the side. He grinned. "I also get to see your drawin's?"

"Yes, as an added bonus, you'll get my ass as well."

His eyes flared and heated. He closed them and swallowed. He leveled me with a gaze full of desire, yet he still asked, "Are you sure your leg's—"

"Shut up. I'm fine. Besides, you'll be doin' all the work to pleasure me."

His smile was wicked. "Yeah, lover, I'll pleasure you in every damn way."

"Then give me a song, Zion," I ordered. Already I was thickening from just watching him. He winked and picked up his guitar. He pulled the chaise lounge away from the end of the bed and sat on it, facing me. With the guitar on his lap, he strummed a few beats, listening to the tone.

I didn't expect how hot he would look sitting shirtless with his fingers strumming over a guitar while looking at me with soft eyes and a small smile. "Any preference in song?"

"You pick," I told him, my tone gentle.

His fingers worked like magic over the notes. He was skilled, more than I thought he would be. My eyes flicked up when he began to sing. My heart stumbled. I quivered from his voice as he sang the first lines of "Human" by Rag'n'Bone Man.

My pulse raced. I didn't expect him to sing along with the guitar. I didn't know he'd have an amazing voice. But he did.

Jesus Christ. I was dating a god.

He was fucking perfect.

His voice faltered over a couple of words when he noticed I'd gone hard. I grabbed a pillow to cover myself because I didn't want him distracted. He continued, and I was lost in watching him.

Hell, my chest hurt with how much this man, *my* man, could make me feel. It wasn't just because he could play and sing. It was just him. Zion had crashed into my world and turned it upside down. He'd adapted to being bisexual easily, even though he would say it was my skills that converted him.

Thank fuck I'd put forward the challenge to suck him off in the first place, and for both of us being stubborn, else I wouldn't be sitting in front of him naked. I wouldn't have his warm eyes on me. I wouldn't have him as mine, and that would be a tragedy.

When he'd finished the song, I wanted him to sing another, then another, but I also wanted something so much more.

"Do you mind if we read and look at my work later?" I asked.

He placed the guitar on the chaise after he stood and turned back to me while undoing the button and zipper on his jeans. "You want me?"

I nodded. "Yeah."

"I'm gonna fuck you, lover."

I swallowed. "Please."

He pushed his jeans and boxers down and kicked them off. "Lay down, Kylo," he ordered, and my dick gave a happy jerk in response to his harder tone.

As I slid down the bed, my breath hitched when he moved the pillow off me and threw it over the side somewhere. Zion walked to the bedside table and pulled the drawer open, setting lube on the bed. The lack of condoms made my heart trip over itself, pleased as hell we'd already discussed our health and how we didn't need to be wrapped up.

Clearing my throat, I watched him kneel on the bed and palm his cock while his heated gaze ran over me. "Tell me," he demanded.

My brows dipped in question. "What?" I asked, my tone soft.

"Tell me what you do with the dildo."

Rolling my eyes, red covered my cheeks. "You already know."

"No." He shook his head. "I might already know, but I wanna hear it outta your sweet mouth, baby."

How could I resist? Even when it embarrassed me, I reached out and ran a hand gently up and down his thigh and said, "There's times I have a need. A need to feel full. It's those times I slather the dildo up and use it to fuck myself so hard I'm lost in the sensation and come like I haven't in years."

"You won't need it anymore… unless I use it on you," he told me, his jaw clenching.

I cocked a brow. "I won't?"

"Fuck no. I'll always be there for any urge you get."

"Then show me," I said.

"Please," Zion clipped.

Fuck me.

"Please," I whispered.

"First, you get my fingers. I want to watch them glide in and out of your tight hole. I wanna see how lost I can get you before you even get my cock. I'll fill you more than any dildo, lover, and you'll take it, wantin' more and more. But only if you're good will I give it to you."

"Okay," I complied.

His grin was smug. I'd let him have it, though, because I loved losing control, and I had a feeling that Zion was starting to understand, and he liked it.

"Spread 'em, Kylo."

I parted my legs, wincing only a little, which Zion didn't catch, thank fuck, else he would have stopped. I didn't want to stop for anything. Zion climbed between my legs. He leaned down and took my mouth in a demanding kiss, and I gave it over to him. I curled my arms around his back and ran my hands up and down over his warm skin.

"Fuck, baby, I can't wait to be in you," he mumbled against my lips before moving down to my neck and chest, where he sucked on my nipple.

"Zion, please," I begged, wanting his touch.

"What do you want, lover?"

"You," I told him through heavy breaths.

He licked down my body, paying attention to my hip with his teeth, tongue, and lips. "Where do you want me?"

"Your fingers in me."

"You'll get it when I say, baby."

I groaned in frustration, my body already begging for release. My cock was so fucking hard and leaking from his attention.

My heart thumped harder over the extra beat when Zion grabbed the lube. I edged my legs apart a little further. Eager, ready, and needy.

I hissed out a breath when he bit down on my hip and pushed a finger inside me. "Yes," I yelled, gripping his shoulders and rocking down on his finger.

My vision blurred when another finger joined the other and ran over my prostate.

"Zion, please, fuck, please, just get in me."

"You want my cock?"

"Yes," I demanded on a yell.

"Lover, you ain't ready."

"I am. Promise, I am."

"When I say, Kylo," he told me, and I grumbled under my breath only to lose that oxygen when he scissored his fingers inside me, stretching me for him.

Later I would question how he knew what to do, but not right then.

"Jesus, baby, you're so tight."

He hovered over me. Unable to resist, I grabbed him, pulling him down and kissing him while I locked my thighs around his lower half and ground my ass down on his fingers.

Zion tore his mouth from mine. "Settle," he demanded.

"I can't. I need—"

"Kylo," he growled.

"But—"

"Do as I say," he clipped.

Grinding my teeth, I unlocked my grip from his shoulders and hips.

Zion smiled, removing his fingers. "Good, baby." He leaned back to his knees and grabbed the lube. "As a reward for listenin', you can have me." He ran lube over his own leaking hard-on. "Roll over," he ordered. With a slight cringe from a pull on my leg, I quickly rolled over like a man on a mission—something Zion found amusing, since he chuckled.

He kissed my lower back. "Love that you do as you're told, lover." He kissed my ass cheek. "Gets me so fuckin' hot." I shifted my legs apart around him as he kissed my other ass cheek. "Christ, you look good spread out for me, your hole callin' to me."

"Zion, please," I begged and jutted my ass back.

He slapped each cheek, causing me to cry out. "Patience, baby." He ran his hands over my ass slowly, like a gentle massage. "Hell, Kylo, fuckin' love your body."

Zion dropped a kiss to my waist, my shoulder, and I glanced over to see him there looking down between our bodies. When I felt his tip nudging against my hole, I knew what he was watching.

I lifted my ass up a little, and the tip of his dick sank in. I gripped the sheets under me when he pushed in slowly, filling me in the best fucking way possible.

"Zion." I moaned his name when he was all the way in and pressing in just the right spot.

"Holy hell, lover. Fuck me, you feel good." He kissed my shoulder again and I got more of his weight when he went to one elbow. He pulled back out of me and pushed in with a groan.

He threaded his fingers from his free hand with mine and held on while his thrusts got a little wild. Sounds fell from my mouth. I loved him inside me. Loved him fucking me.

"Yes, fuck, Zion, you feel good."

Groaning, he rested his forehead against my back for a moment while he fucked my ass like it hadn't been before. It felt different with him. Better. More intense. He placed a kiss to my shoulder. Needing more, I tipped my head back a little and he pressed against me to kiss me.

My dick rubbed into the bed, giving me the friction I needed while Zion's cock pushed, rubbed, and slid in the perfect way.

"Zion," I cried, clutching at the sheets. "Close," I warned.

"Me too, baby, me too. You feel fuckin' fantastic. Christ." His thrusts weren't in any rhythm; they were frantic, just lost to the feel, to the pleasure.

My body tensed for a second as my balls drew up. I tightened around him and rubbed my cock into the sheets as the first wave hit me. My cum shot out over the bed, my ass clenched around Zion, and I heard him grunt, then groan. His grip on my hip squeezed, and finally, he thickened inside me, the warmth of his cum filling me and feeling so damn right.

"Fuck," he clipped, his forehead resting onto my back even as his hips pistoned in and out at a fast pace. His orgasm sent mine into a longer one, and by the time both of us were coming down, we panted out our breaths.

"Jesus motherfuckin' Christ," Zion said as he slowly slid out of me, causing me to shudder, and flopped down beside me on the bed. His arm and leg curved over me, hugging me close to him as we took in the extra oxygen we needed. "Lover, that was somethin' fuckin' special."

Hell, that was just what I'd been thinking.

"Agreed." I smiled.

He grinned back and leaned in for a kiss.

Some tension that I didn't really want to register I had left me. So maybe I'd been worried about his reaction, feeling weird over having me for the first time. But hearing him call it special... meant the damn world to me.

Just like he did.

"Kylo," Zion growled. "If you don't get the fuck up here, I'll rip your dick off—shit, I won't. Unlatch your motherfuckin' teeth, lover. Yeah, baby, that's better. You know I wouldn't rip off the part I love most—fuck, I love all of you."

Zion's dick dropped from my mouth. "Wait, what?"

His hooded eyes gleamed down at me. "I ain't just sayin' it because your teeth are close to my dick, but I do love you, Kylo."

Christ.

Jesus Christ.

My body heated, my heart pounded, my pulse raced.

He loved me.

Zion Storey loved *me*.

Yeah, we'd been dating for a while, but I didn't expect him to blurt out the "I love you." Still, it was how I felt for him, and he needed to know.

Climbing up his body, I lay over him. He smiled softly, wrapping his arms around my waist. I was surprised he didn't grind up against my hardness with his own, but he just watched me.

He took my weight easily and brushed hair from my face before cupping my cheek. "You mean everything to me," he told me.

My body hummed. I licked my lips, and then said, "You know I love you too, right?"

His smile grew. "I know."

I rolled my eyes, my insides feeling light. "Cocky."

"You like it."

I shook my head. "I love it."

"Move in with me?"

He'd been asking me for the last couple of months, and I'd said no each time. Even when he'd moved into his new digs, which were sweet. However, I couldn't say no any longer, because he was my future.

"Sure."

His eyes flashed. "Yeah?"

"Yes, Zion. I'll move in with you."

He whooped before rolling over and taking my mouth in a slow but hot kiss. He pulled back. "I didn't hurt your leg?"

Smiling, I shook my head. "Stop askin' that. You know it's doin' a lot better."

He kissed my jaw, my neck, my shoulder. "I can't help it. I worry about you like a little old lady does about her pets."

"Are you callin' me a pet?" I asked.

He chuckled. "Maybe. But a cute pet." He pecked my mouth. "A sweet pet." He took my bottom lip between his teeth and bit down. Letting go, he ran his tongue across the sensitive flesh. "A sexy pet who will fuck his master?"

My heart was already hammering in my chest because it was Zion and he'd driven my body crazy with every touch. But it kicked up into a speed a race car driver would be surprised by.

"You want me to fuck you?"

He hummed under his breath.

"Slide my cock in your ass?" I asked.

He rubbed his hard cock against mine, his knees dropping to the bed beside my hips. I gripped his ass tightly and moaned.

"I'll do it." Of fucking course I would. "But don't expect me to call you master."

He harrumphed but followed with "Fine. But maybe on a few occasions?"

"I won't—"

"I'll sing to you more."

Fucking hell.

"I'll think about it."

He chuckled. "Knew that would work."

"Zion, you could become a star with your voice."

He shook his head. "Not somethin' I'm after. I'm just happy bein' the star in your eyes."

I shoved at him and snorted. "Fuckin' hell, you're corny."

"You like it," he said.

Again, I shook my head and said, "I love it."

The humor dancing in his eyes left. "You woke me up in the best damn way, or I would have lost out on havin' this with you. Know it won't be fantastic all the time. Know we'll argue, but I need you to know I'll do everythin' I can to make sure you'll be sleepin' at my side. That you'll still love me until we're fuckin' old. That's how serious I am with you."

Holy shit.

My organs were rejoicing with one another in the center of my body. I cupped his cheek and said softly, "I'm right there with you, Zion."

"Good." Then his smile was back. "Can't thank you enough for offerin' up to suck me off that first time."

Lightly laughing, I pulled him close and told him, "You're welcome."

"Now, are you gonna pleasure me, lover?"

"Oh yeah, in a way that'll blow your mind."

He lowered his head and kissed me. Blindly reaching out, I grabbed the tube of lube, opened it, and squirted some onto my fingers. As Zion got me hot with his mouth, I reached between the gap and gently ran my fingers over his puckered hole. He sighed against my lips. It surprised me he wanted this, but then again, he surprised me a lot over the time we'd been together.

He pushed back on my fingers and I slowly inserted one. He stilled for a moment, but then relaxed and kissed me harder, our tongues dancing against one another's. I withdrew the finger and pushed back in with two. He groaned against my lips.

We stayed like that for a while, so I could stretch him, get him ready for me. Each time I played with his prostate, he would lift his ass up on my fingers and make noises in the back of his throat.

Christ, I would never get over how Zion was mine and how damn hot he was.

He pulled back, both of us breathing heavily. "Need you, baby," he said, his tone rough.

"Then you've got me." I'd already rubbed lube onto my hard-on, so I tapped his thighs and said, "Lift a little."

He did. Reaching between us, I took hold of my cock and rested it against Zion's hole.

"Relax for me, sweetheart," I ordered and witnessed his eyes heating even more when I used an endearment. "Good," I said when he took a breath, and slowly, I started to slide up inside his tight ass.

Wrapping my hand around his erection, I moved my fist up and down his length. He groaned, and I slid past the barrier. He closed his eyes and sucked in a sharp breath, pausing.

"It's okay. You're good. Just take it easy."

He nodded and shifted down on me a little more. His hands pressed into my shoulders as he held himself up. I used my free hand to run up and down his thigh and waist.

"Fuck, babe, you feel fuckin' good. So good, Christ," I muttered.

As soon as I was all the way in, Zion stopped moving and opened his eyes. He blew out a shaky breath. "Not sure what the hype is—fucking hell, Jesus Christ, again," he yelled when I'd rocked my dick against the right spot. I did it again, and his whole body tensed around me. His ass squeezed my dick harder, and hell, I loved it.

Taking his waist in both hands, I lifted him slowly and then pulled him back down, making sure I pressed against his prostate.

"Yeah, fuck yeah, Kylo."

Soon enough, Zion took back control, and he rode me like he'd done it a million times before. His eyes stayed locked onto mine until he dipped and took my mouth in a hot kiss. Our tongues and bodies danced together in ways that had me feeling so damn much. I wrapped my arms around Zion, dug my feet into the mattress, and even when my leg twinged, I lifted his hips and thrust up into him. He stilled, groaned, and kissed me harder. I did it again and again, knowing my body slipped closer to its release.

Zion broke the kiss. "Fuck, I'm close."

"Me too," I said, cupping his face before sliding my thumb into his mouth where he sucked it. I moaned and grunted when he bit down and groaned around my thumb as his ass clamped around my cock and hot jets of semen warmed my stomach from his climax. I couldn't hold back; I couldn't stop it. His release dragged out mine and I pumped my cum into his ass.

Zion collapsed on top of me, his nose gently swiping up my cheek. He breathed heavily as he said, "I'll get off soon."

I snorted. "You already did."

He chuckled. "Yeah, baby, I did. Can't understand why all men aren't out there gettin' their asses fucked. Hell, that was damn powerful."

"Told you."

"You did." He leaned in and kissed my cheek before gently moving off me and to my side. "You make me giddy inside, Kylo. Fuckin' giddy. How fucked up is that?"

Turning my head, I smiled at him. "Not stupid, just because we're guys doesn't mean we can't feel giddy over each other."

"We're hardass bikers. Giddy shouldn't be in our vocab."

"Bullshit. Not when we got love between us."

"Yeah, that's true." He got to his elbow and stared down at me with a grin. "You're movin' in with me."

I smiled up at him. "I am."

"Love you, Kylo."

Running a hand up his chest, I told him, "And I fuckin' love you, Zion, but I still won't call you master."

He threw his head back and laughed. When he finally calmed, he leaned in and pressed his lips against mine. There, he said, "I'll wear you down."

Hell, he probably would. I'd do anything for Zion Storey.

ACKNOWLEDGMENTS

A massive thank you to the doctors, nurses, and everyone who's helping out through the pandemic.

It's been such hard times throughout the world. I know I wasn't the only one scared. I know I wasn't the only one worried about everything going on. I also know I wasn't the only one who would have picked up a book to get lost in so the real world and concerns would disappear even for a moment. I hope things are settling down for everyone, but still, make sure to take care and stay safe!

Thank you to my Muffkateers (readers group) and everyone who has picked up a copy of *Never a Saint*.

Jay at Designs by Juan, you always outdo yourself with each cover we work on together!

My family, thank you for your support. You all mean everything to me.

There is always a thank you to Becky at Hot Tree Editing. You make my life easier, and I seriously love working with you!!

To my beta team: Lindsey, Amanda. B, Darlene, Nikki, Miranda, Amanda. E, Annissia, Casey, and Allena.

Romantic Comedies

Making Changes

Making Sense

Fumbled Love

Trinity Love Series

Left to Chance (m/m/f novel)

Love of Liberty (m/m/f novella)

<u>TITLES UNDER **L. ROSE**</u>

The Hidden Kingdom Trilogy

A Torn Paige

A Lost Paige

A Final Paige

CONNECT WITH LILA ROSE

Web page: https://www.lilarosebooks.com/

Facebook: http://bit.ly/2du0taO

Instagram: https://www.instagram.com/lilarose78/?hl=en